# Girl of the Golden West

# Girl of the Golden West

A novel
## JULIA WHEDON

Charterhouse
New York

## GIRL OF THE GOLDEN WEST

Second Printing, May 1973

Whedon

LIBRARY OF CONGRESS CATALOG CARD NUMBER: 72-95172
MANUFACTURED IN THE UNITED STATES OF AMERICA

FOR DICK

". . . the fundamental fact is
that there's no such thing as
a grown up person . . ."

Malraux
*Anti-Memoirs*

# Girl of the Golden West

# 1

I checked the weather in *The New York Times*. Los Angeles: partly cloudy and in the eighties. Same in Madrid, Lisbon, and Chicago. It was raining in Moscow, wouldn't you know.

No one seemed the least surprised by my precipitous journey. The doorman merely nodded and said he'd hold my mail. The clerk at the airline had no trouble booking me on a flight—even with so little notice. I was supposed to be dining at Lutèce that evening with friends, yet when I called to cancel they said they understood perfectly. How come? I wasn't given to flying off to places without warning. I hadn't been back to L.A. since I was a kid. Now, all at once, I had to be there immediately.

I wasn't prepared. I don't believe in doing anything immediately. And it did seem to me if you were going to change climates and time zones, oceans even, the least you could do was zip out to Bloomingdale's and buy something wrinkle-resistant. If only as a gesture. One should observe transitions, I feel, as a courtesy to fate, particularly before flying through the air.

But there simply wasn't time, and before I knew it I was airborne. We did not take off when they said we would, of course. The wait on the runway was twice as long as they announced it would be. Nor did they show the movie they said they were going to show. Just as I began to feel restless and deceived, they instructed me to keep my seatbelt fastened at all times, for my own "comfort." Then they started throwing things at me like smoked nuts and Chicken Wellington (which I'm sure doesn't exist) and, of course, booze in little dolly bottles.

Disoriented and docile, as programmed, I shored myself up with a number of small pillows and plugged myself into the miracle of in-flight stereo. Extravagant Strauss broke over my poor beleaguered eardrums as we bounced across the clouds, followed by foot-tapping fox trots, and French lessons for the severely brain-damaged. Then, finally, a dubbed Italian comedy was shown on a screen the size of a mailing envelope. Might that be the Wasatch Range below, I asked the stewardess. She really wouldn't know, she said, with that little smile that implied she was a customer, not a salesgirl.

Mercifully the movie ended, as did our flight. The human feedlot was off-loaded. My senses were so blunted by all the jet-stream hospitality, I didn't have the requisite muscular coordination to get my baggage off the carousel. Three times it passed me by, three times I waited for it to reappear.

All airport interiors are alike. You could be anywhere. It wasn't until I stepped out of the terminal that I realized they'd varied the geography. Three spindly palms stood at the far side of the parking lot. It really *was* California. My heart began to pound. I reset my watch. I had to retreat three hours. Oh well, only one more cocktail hour to go.

I claimed my rented car (which is sort of like meeting

a blind date) and headed, I hoped, for Pacific Palisades and the home of Gene and Sally Fox, nice people I hadn't seen in three years. I didn't have the guts to stay at the Bel Air, so I called the Foxes (he had formerly been my agent before moving to the Coast with another agency) and they said sure, stay as long as you like.

My palms were damp and my breath was tight. I was following instructions I had gotten at the airport: Century Boulevard to the Santa Monica Freeway. Freeways were a gag to me: *Why do you know they drive so fast on those Freeways . . . Those Freeways are so crowded I once saw a man . . .* quickies in a Bob Hope monologue. They had all been built since I had left years ago. Pounding towards the Pacific with ruthless efficiency, not recognizing anything, I suddenly saw a sign: Beverly Hills Next Three Exits. The thought was like seagulls to a sailor. If I could just get there . . .

Beginning four years before, with what had been a very discreet little nervous breakdown (it looked a lot like the flu) I started writing a book. Oh. First a word or two about the breakdown. It wasn't a class-A affair. It didn't take three strong men to hold me down, and I didn't try to hurt myself. I just didn't go outside for six weeks. I consulted a friend about medical assistance and she said "why don't you wait 'til you're a little bit sicker?" She had a point. And, too, the metaphors are so tedious. I knew how I got the way I was, it was just a question of what I was going to do about it. All this was a result of eight years of graduate studies and idiot jobs doing "research" for a magazine and a network. It all seemed so meaningless. I decided it would be better to sell stockings at Bloomingdale's than pretend to be significantly involved in glamour jobs. But when I went

3

to apply, they said I was over-qualified. They insisted I go into their executive training program. I told them I didn't want to make it my life's work and that my abundant qualifications would make me a super salesgirl. But they said they knew better.

I wandered on to the main floor, drifted into Notions, and broke into a glistening sweat. Hot tears bounced down my cheeks. In some way my feelings were desperately hurt, like a seven-year-old whose stolen bike reveals to her the infinite wickedness of the world that nobody ever bothered to mention.

There was a terrible chasm outside my building that prevented me from going out. If I crossed it, I became faint, frightened, sweaty. I tried over and over but couldn't make it. But boredom egged me on. I felt like Friday on that Island, fashioning ways to live.

I ordered everything by phone which was hard because you have trouble visualizing those freezer cases. I stole magazines from the garbage room—and one from somebody's pile of mail. But only because I was so desperate. I tried to make friends in the building. I taught myself origami and watched the Soaps. But being crazy is terribly boring.

I hit upon the idea of writing a book in order to appear busy to myself, and not crazy. A thoroughly crazy person could not pursue a rational narrative, said I, maniacally attending to the writing of my book. After a while the book began to interest me. We don't live out our lives in paragraphs and chapters but it helped me to shape my life. A *crise de nerfs* is no giggling matter.

I began with the facts because they were immediate and moving to me. But soon I began to write fiction. Things began to move all by themselves. It was like see-

4

ing a child take a step and then another. Or getting a joke for the first time. Or learning to whistle. It was fantastic and—shaft of sunlight, up chorus, hands around—I was well again!

Then, just to add irony to absurdity, the stupid book sold. And got decent reviews. Barbara Walters, who never interviews first novelists, interviewed me on the "Today" show—right after a man who invented the world's largest gong. Then some goon optioned it for the movies. And suddenly people were talking about screenplays, and money, and percentages, and I couldn't understand a thing they were talking about. So I decided: screw it! No more phone calls. I'd fly to the coast. It all seemed terribly excessive. There is something about despair that cheapens euphoria, assuming it ever follows.

Driving down Sunset after all those years of forgetting, and remembering, and finally writing about it—it was as if I were tunneling backward. Nothing had changed. Just for a moment I wondered if life could resume where it had left off.

# 2

There must have been twenty people in the room. I was having trouble keeping my mind on what anyone was saying. I smiled and repeated myself briefly on a few safe topics. Yes, New York was all they said it was. No, I wouldn't be staying more than a week. Such a shame, yes. My eyes traveled around the room. A carpet of silvery green eddied around the legs of a giant white coffee table and a couch covered with handwoven fabric full of mustard colored lumps. Glass gave way to atrium, to landscape, to canyon, to sea, in a seemingly endless series of perspectives. Even within, the women seemed like some botanical manifestation. Evening pajamas, skirts and slacks abounded in brilliant primary colors like zinnias. The men were tan and talked mostly to each other.

The conversation was about Common Cause, the Governor, today's air, and tennis scores. I asked someone if he liked his Tensor racket. Really shows up in the serve. Did I get in much tennis back East? No I didn't, darn. There was a whole New York answer to that question involving rape, robbery, park permits, roof clubs, but I was glad of the chance to duck it. I was feeling a little like the lady from Borneo as it was. Sally led me away.

"I bet you're tired," Sally said, taking my glass. "It usually takes Gene two days to make the switch." A maid offered us an assortment of sliced brioche with mayonnaise and onion slices, and potted shrimp with dill on dark rounds.

"Oh," Sally said, licking a finger, "I meant to tell you. It turns out we have a mutual friend. Nick Ballard."

"For heaven's sake," I said, so surprised I felt dizzy for a moment.

"He said he hadn't seen you in years—"

"Not since I was a kid. How is he?"

"Just great. Gene knows him through business, of course. And we all like tennis. You know the courts over in Rustic Canyon?"

"That's since my time—that was all bramble, or a polo field, or something."

"I asked Nick to come tonight but he couldn't make it," Sally said, wiping a wet ring off a table. "But we'll work out something. He said he's dying to see you. You won't have to go back right away, will you?"

"I hope not. It really depends on how all this business stuff goes. It could take a week or so."

"Aren't you excited?" Sally smiled.

"You know, I'm actually more excited about being in California than I am about the movie. It's been so long."

"How long?"

"Twenty years."

"I don't believe it! I had no idea—I thought from the book—"

"I made it all up."

7

"You're a cheat. Well, I think you'll find it very changed. Westwood is full of skyscrapers."

"You know what? I'd know it anywhere. From what I could see coming in from the airport—everything is the same, just more so. And when I saw those crazy oil wells with those dust covers on them, I thought I'd cry, I was so glad to see them."

"You really do like California," Sally mused. "You're one of the few, you know."

"I adore it."

"I wonder," Sally said all at once, "Could I ask you a favor?"

"Sure."

"Annie wants you to see something and begged me to ask you—it would just take a minute. She's almost ready for bed, but she gets so excited when we have company."

"Of *course*. Where is she?"

"Out by the pool."

"I'm on my way," I said, really perfectly happy to consult with Annie.

"I'll freshen this," Sally said, taking my glass. "Down the hall and to the left. Don't slip on the stair."

I padded down the white terrazo hall. Filmy curtains moved restlessly in a fresh breeze off the ocean. The stone floor looked so cool. I took off my shoes. It was cool. I passed a powder room and thought to use it as long as it was there. A large ironstone sea shell filled with sherbet colored soaps sat on the counter. The basin was like a dimple in the marble surface, and smoke-tinted mirror rose from sink to ceiling all around. I lifted my head and looked at myself while the water ran cool over my wrists. I was used to my mirror at home. It gave a frank reply to my question. This mirror seemed to make

8

constructive suggestions, as if it were trying to sell me
something. The tawny lipstick is nice but goes better with
pavement, don't you think? Might we suggest just a
touch of sun? And the black top—warm colors are so
much nicer. I took a long look at my ribbed body stock-
ing and low-slung pants, the heavy swaying watch chain.
I thought of all those soft-spoken anemones in the other
room. Gee whiz, darn it, golly. I looked like somebody's
jailer. Shit. I stuck my tongue out at myself and continued my journey down the hall.

I passed a Picasso lithograph, a Miró, a Klee, a Ben
Shahn, a wooden head from the Pacific Islands, old and
splintery, an urn full of dried flowers; three steps down
and there was the pool.

It was painted black, which made the water look navy
blue. The water recirculated through a spout that you
could hear gently peeing in the distance. Near the shallow end was a giant black dish filled with volcanic rock.
A flame, fed by a gas jet at the bottom, danced harm-
lessly about the jagged black rocks. Annie, small and
dark, lay by the pool telling herself something.

"Hiya," I called out so she would know I was there.

"Hi," she said, sitting up. "Did Mommy send you out
here?"

"I sort of wanted to come out anyway. I was wonder-
ing where you were. You look really nice in that dress."

"It's a mumu."

"Ahh. A mumu. I wonder what that means . . ."

"A kind of a dress, I guess," Annie said shrugging.

"Sounds right. From Hawaii?"

"My Uncle Nick brought it back," she said proudly.

"Your uncle is a good buyer," I observed. Polished
cotton—green shot with lavender—it was exactly right

9

against her brown skin and thick black hair. You could see what she was going to be.

"Do your shirt tails go all the way to the bottom?" Annie asked.

"They do."

"The kind that don't come out?"

"Right."

"They're really good, aren't they?"

"They really are," I said, managing to conceal my amusement. She was perfectly right. They were really good. We sat by the pool quietly listening to the wind stir in the trees. There are no soft incidental sounds in a city. Annie swushed the water with her bare arm, causing it to slurp later in the gutters.

"Would you care for a Frito?" Annie asked, passing me a saucer. "I have my very own cocktail. See?" she said, holding up a glass filled with Coke and ice. "Where's your drink?"

"Your mother's fixing me one."

"I bet she isn't. See? She's talking." She pointed to the living room which looked, from where we were sitting, like a display window. There was Sally kissing and being kissed. The room had filled up considerably since I had left. I'd have to face them all when I went back in. It was like bailing water.

"Well," I said, getting up off the ground, "I guess I better go back in and be delightful. Do you envy me?"

"I'm not such a good talker," Annie confessed uncomfortably.

"Me either."

"Want to see something?"

"Sure."

Annie took a long match stick, lit it from the brazier,

10

and lit the wicks on a fleet of floating candles. One by one she launched them gently in the pool. She doused the match with a hiss in the water and watched the candles, her chin on her knee.

"That's my favorite thing in the whole world. I wish I never had to go to sleep."

"Annie. Bed. *Annie?*" Sally called in the distance.

"Coming! Here," she said handing me the matches, "don't let the lights go out. Do you think they'll burn all night?"

"I'll let you know. Night, Annie."

"Night," she said, and went inside.

Annie reminded me of myself. The injustice of bedtime. Who could forget? It wasn't until she left that I realized I wanted to be alone. Away from the party. Just for a moment.

I walked around the side of the house where there were no lights, no voices, nothing to subvert the timelessness of that western night. The crickets were nagging. My pulse began to bound. I picked my way down the steep, shrub-covered hill that dropped away from the Foxes' house. Dry sharp twigs scraped against my bare arms. My scalp shivered. This was far enough. I stopped. You aren't really supposed to leave parties and adult conversation and sit in the weeds when you're over thirty. Also, you go forward in time, not backward. I wiped a trickle of blood from a cut and tasted it. Turning to the wind, so it split evenly across my face, I breathed deeply, almost to a sob. Juniper, jacaranda, monkey tails, willow, sage, laurel, poison oak, snails, look out for tics, rattlers, mica, eucalyptus. And Nick. Sure, count him, too.

11

# 3

The smell of the heat in the ground at the end of the day. How well I remember. And the aroma of weeds and bushes and your own jeans, strong as tea—God, what a feeling. Not five miles away—but years and years ago, I used to play in hills, like these, that rose behind our house. Somewhere else the afternoon may have lingered, but when the sun slid behind the rim of our canyon, it plunged us into evening. The ground and foliage turned dark purples, browns, and black. The sky, with the first bold evening stars, stayed blue as the water in a grotto. For a while. Then, when you could no longer tell who was a cowboy and who was an Indian, it was time to go in.

We slipped and slid down the hill, cursing the burrs, exploding soft charges of milkweed, until we reached the gully at the bottom. As the last of us came crashing down out of the underbrush, we started walking up the arroyo. The ground was hard and baked into patterns the sudden rushing water had left. We laid plans for the next day.

"I got Sunday School tomorrow," Kyle announced.

"Can't you get out of it?"

12

"Are you kidding?"

"Which one you go to?" Toby asked.

"Latter-Day Saints. In Santa Monica," Kyle mumbled.

"Aw, too bad. I thought maybe it was Saint Alban's. I figured if it was Saint Alban's I might come with you."

"What's so good about Saint Alban's?"

"They give you a robe and let you sing in the choir first time," Toby said.

Everybody thought about that one for awhile. Not a bad deal.

"Well, I wouldn't wanta sing in a choir anyhow. That's for sissies."

"Is not," said Toby.

"Is."

"I just remembered—I can't play tomorrow either," Billy said. "I gotta go to a cook-out. My cousin is coming in from Pasadena," he said, heaving a rock sideways as if to skip it across the water.

"Lucky," someone said.

"You should see my cousin from Pasadena. She has these huge freckles and fat kinky pigtails and her bathing suit shows everything."

"P.U.," Toby said.

"You want to play tomorrow?" I asked Benjie, seeing everyone else was busy.

"I'll have to ask my mother first," he said.

"Well *natch*," I said.

Benjie wasn't the best boy I knew, or anything, but he was pretty okay. And he had some neat toys. He was an only child, as my mother kept pointing out all the time, and was sort of spoiled. But not in a bad way. But anyhow, because he had asthma, his parents were always

13

giving him toys. He had so many small cars he had them parallel-parked on his shelves. This struck me as a masterpiece of organization and civility in one so young. By contrast, my yo-yo was usually buried under a pile of underpants in my shirt drawer.

"Hey, Benjie, your fly's open," Kyle said.

"Big deal," Benjie said, yanking up the zipper. "Swell: now my underpants are stuck in it."

"So maybe Katie'll fix it for you. Ha-ha," Kyle teased and ran down the gully towards his house.

"You're a real stinker, Kyle, and everybody knows it!" I yelled after him.

The crickets were throbbing and there was a chill in the air. It was getting late. We all ran home.

I scaled the retaining wall and ran fast under the fruit trees. It was creepy at night stepping on an orange or lemon that had fallen, over-ripe, to the ground. They felt like living things and scared me.

I sprinted and dodged across the orchard. I could hear the sprinkler throwing out ropes of water across the lawn. The lights from the house showed me what to do. I got the rhythm and ran between the liquid arcs, without getting caught.

"You left your bike out again," my father said without saying hello. "No radio tonight."

That stern voice of responsibility. It had long since gone inward, but it was nothing more than a cheap impersonation of my father's voice. It brought me instantly to my feet.

"What do you mean by sitting in the bushes after dark? If I've told you once, I've told you a hundred times . . ." it was saying even now.

14

"I'm coming, I'm coming. Just five more minutes?"

*"Now,"* it said.

Reluctantly, I headed back up the hill toward the Foxes.

# 4

I wonder whatever became of my feeling for parties. God knows I used to look forward to them. The preparations were so elaborate and far-reaching, like something out of a nineteenth-century novel. There was shining, and polishing, and buffing, and mulching. There were flower arrangements to be made, and bathrooms to be scrubbed. Potatoes to peel, and peas to shell. A man came and left an entire case of Scotch! We unpacked the groceries and there would be a dozen bags of potato chips, bottles of collins mixer, anchovy paste, minced clams, angostura bitters, all right in with our regular groceries (which were necessarily restricted because of rationing). We made extra ice and I whipped bowl after bowl of dismal adult foods. Dear God, the sights I saw: pureed peas, fish—served with grapes. Artichokes trimmed and served cold. Cooked mushrooms and kidneys. *Kidneys*. Actual organs taken from inside—I mean they'd *eat* them. So these were the things adults preferred. This is what they did together. . . .

"Put the pink one in the bathroom, dear," Mother said, handing me a stack of ashtrays. (Jesus, they even smoked in the bathroom.) "And one on the piano for Nick, in case he wants to play."

I picked out the nicest one for Nick. It was glass and had frozen bubbles in it. He was my favorite person. I hoped, I hoped, I *hoped* he would play.

We rearranged furniture indoors and outdoors. Mother put a stack of records on the machine—Crosby, Stafford, King Cole, Dinah, Astaire. In two hours they'd begin to slap down and play. I retired to my room—since everything else had been declared off limits. I chose my very best nightie to wear. I would be allowed to stay up for a little while if I was very-good-and-polite-and-didn't-bother-the-guests.

The nightie I chose was a yellow one with eyelet and a yellow sash that dropped almost to the floor. I was learning to iron at the time and had spent twenty minutes getting it just right.

I thrust my jeans and T-shirt into the hamper, washed my face and hands, and began to brush my hair hard. It was thick and auburn and full of burrs. All the blood ran down to my elbows and made my arms ache. I cursed and tried again. It was no use. I couldn't get them out. Suddenly, for no apparent reason, I began to cry. I threw my brush to the floor with a loud crack.

"What the hell's going on in there?" I heard my father call from my parents' bedroom. My mother came into the bathroom. "What is it?" she said sternly.

"I hate parties," I cried, "and I've got burrs in my hair."

She sighed, looked at her watch, and took me into her bedroom. She sat me down at her dressing table and brushed my hair for me. She had to cut loose some of the burrs.

17

"You know, if you wouldn't roll in the dirt it would help."

"I don't roll in the dirt. Who'd want to do a thing like *that*," I said defensively.

"Well, whatever it is you do. Look, try and remember you're a girl. Okay?"

"*Okay*," *s*aid, looking down at my lap. All at once I felt a chill mist settle on my shoulders. I looked up. Cologne. Mother doused herself and put her earrings on.

"Come on. We still have stuff to do," she said, heading out the door. I liked the way her dress sounded. We both smelled terrific.

Soon the doorbell began to ring. It was sudden, and very loud, like overture music. This was it! It scared the hell out of me. The first people to arrive were the Carpenters. We had a family bet on that they would be. They lived down the street from us and we had, in fact, seen them that same afternoon pricing garden furniture at Bullocks. It seemed very odd now seeing them all dressed up. And nobody said a word about seeing one another earlier. Then Mrs. Carpenter, who was always telling me not to step in her geraniums, was saying to me *my*, didn't I look *lovely*. I wanted to say something adroit about her dress but I really hated it.

After a while Mr. Carpenter offered her a cigarette and lit it. Mrs. Carpenter inhaled and then exhaled to one side. She wondered how I was enjoying school. Was she kidding? She seemed very nervous. So was I. I ran out to the kitchen.

"Holy smoke, Mom, nobody's saying anything in there."

"They will," she said calmly, removing some bubbling cheese triangles from the oven.

18

"Yeah, but if everybody knows each other already, what are they going to talk about? I mean, I can see talking if you're getting up sides for a game or something."

Mother was right. People did begin to talk. More people kept coming through the door. Nick Ballard came late, as usual. But he made a big fuss, in a nice way, and I liked that fine. I passed all the dips to him first. He probably didn't even notice. I mean, you couldn't expect a full-grown person to notice what some little eight-year-old did. Could you?

Coats were piled on top of the bed in the master bedroom. Women bent over me smelling like gardenias and lilies and roses. Tanned men shook my hand and said wry things to me I didn't get. Nick whispered in my ear "How's my girl?" and I was so flattered I couldn't answer. I looked around at the house with all its fresh towels, and polished silver, and soft candlelight flickering, and I couldn't help but think what nice people we must be.

Standing in the Foxes' living room now, I had to wonder: why hadn't I turned into one of those fragrant ladies stooping and smiling and saying appropriate things? It was my turn. This party was for me. But I was just lousy at it. I could never figure out what to say. A lifelong shyness made me dry up in front of interesting and attractive people. And the boring ones had me all to themselves. I am an habitual listener and spectator. It has its moments but it's also a kind of bondage. The woman facing me now, for instance, understandably mistook my listening for interest, and was telling me how radical surgery had changed her life. Now she practiced organic gardening, made her own bread, and drank raw milk.

Her skin was smooth as yogurt and her soft myopic gaze was undisturbed by any intelligence whatsoever. She spoke of vitamins in mega-units and bathed, I think she said, in sour cream. A giant blintz!

Gene rescued me from a detailed account of Yogic breathing and kept me moving. The people were mostly very nice and it certainly wasn't their fault I was such a dud. The time difference had really caught up with me. I longed just to go to bed. Lucky Annie.

The party ended around ten. We cleaned up and had some chili and beer. The Foxes saw how punchy I was and sent me off to bed. Such nice people. The sheets on my bed had big yellow flowers on them. So nice. I slept as if I'd been bludgeoned.

# 5

Someone really ought to compose music for "hold." It would make telephoning ever so much more pleasant and I nominate Hugo Winterhalter for the job. Ron Wechsler, the agent handling the deal on the Coast, had me stacked with two other calls for at least ten minutes. Finally, I got permission to land and we made plans to meet at a "great little spot" called the Via Appia.

I guided my oversized sedan with a torn sheet of instructions taped to the horn. I threaded my way through drives, Freeways, exits and a good deal of basic Spanish vocabulary to make it to our rendezvous.

The restaurant was the current rage, for reasons best understood by Californians perhaps. It featured mandolin music (both frantic and wistful), red felt table coverings, baroque gold dishes (which they snapped up as soon as you sat down), campaign stools with tassels and velvet cushions, and giant napkins folded in the origami manner. Mine was a bird.

Our surroundings, as diverting as they were, were no more decorative than the appearance of my agent. He had the plain face, say, of a druggist, but his hair ran in a smooth crest sideways across his forehead in bold defiance of gravity. And lustrous sideburns too he had, detailed like the capital letters in illuminated manuscripts. And withal, rough out slacks nipped in around the vital parts, relenting slightly around the ankles. His shirt was made from party dress fabric, but cut for a mule driver. And resting on his standard hairy chest was a chain with two gold medals, more haberdashery than High Church I should think. He had rings on his fingers (and for all I know, bells on his toes) and a tin ear for newly minted drug talk, which he finally dropped after a couple of drinks. Next, we had onion soup with Zwiebach and something that looked like melted bubble gum floating on top, baked manicotti served in individual chafing dishes ("very hot plate, very hot plate," the waiter warned—not a word about the very cold manicotti). All this was followed by a Caesar salad (Hail!) and combustible cherries of some kind.

As we spoke about this and that, it bothered me that I could not grasp his identity. To all appearances he was bristling with it, but there were no distinguishing marks on his personality. Since I was entrusting him with my affairs, it was a source of some anxiety to me. Downside risks, step-deals, percentages, and front money notwithstanding, was it a good idea to allow yourself to be advised by a person who dressed like a freak, whined like a four-year-old, and drank Coke with his pasta?

"Ron," I seemed to be saying, "I don't understand all this shit."

He looked at me in some astonishment. "Well, I wouldn't say it was shit."

"Well, sure it is. You know, it doesn't really have anything to do with what it is, whether it's any good or not, that kind of thing." There was a long pause.

22

"Well, I may not be a writer, but I certainly consider myself a creative person. People can be gifted with numbers, you know. I mean knowing what your priorities are, what you're willing to give away. A man like Norman Lodeman has to be handled," he said, referring to the producer interested in my book.

"I'm sure you're right. I didn't mean to be rude. You know what I'd like to ask you?"

"What?" he asked, still looking a little injured.

"Do you think it's a good idea?"

"What?"

"Making a picture out of this book."

"I think it has real commercial possibilities."

"But do you think it would make a good picture?"

"Would I be breaking my ass if I didn't?" he said, lending the subject its true value.

"I am worried about the people. The characters. I am worried about their safe passage. Who will be in charge of that?"

"Look, we're still a long way from a deal, but if you're signed to do the adaptation—"

"What if they wreck it?" I said flatly.

"Oh, please. This isn't twenty years ago. This is now. You can make a personal statement. Let it all hang out."

"How about tucking it all back in?" I suggested lamely. It must have been the rum. Magellan's Folly, it was called. It was served with pomegranate seeds.

"We're making strong pictures now that are really relevant to a very heavy audience. We're making a contribution. A cat like Lodeman—did you see *Alive, Black, and With It*? Fantastic. He's a very aware guy."

It didn't take me long to figure out I had Ron worried. Business was slow and it looked like I might gum up the works. I assured him I wouldn't interfere. I thanked him for dinner. He thanked me for coming. The whole thing came to sixty-five dollars and some change. We both took out our little books and deducted each other.

# 6

Driving back to the Palisades, I felt my mind spinning like a centrifuge trying to separate what was me, what was the book, what was the movie. And how many removes from reality were all three? The people I had written about were real (that is, if you believe that memory serves). And, my memories were the premise for the events I projected. But, then, all the projections had come to feel very real too. I mean, if you're a writer and trying at all, it *has* to seem real. The characters' credibility makes them acceptable to your imagination. But the trouble is, soon they start to pass as actual people in small ways. You know, for instance, how they would react to situations you never bothered to devise. They are more affecting than real people because of their rapturous attention, their exquisite responsiveness to your every wish and whim. Writers are liars and dreamers. They are getting away with something every day of their lives. I have a Yankee's respect for the plain truth, and this other side of my character made me very jumpy. And all this talk about a movie was not helping. I mean—what if you were making a serious attempt to be cold sober and looked up and saw Natalie Wood dragging around as

25

you? I mean me? Christ! That would be really sick. Well, Candice Bergen then . . . no, too stiff. *Jesus*, see what happens?

I concentrated on the driving again. *Stella by Starlight* came pleading out of the radio. I sang along for a while. The night was warm and clear. The road curved gracefully left, and then right, dropping into canyons, and rising up again. The houses with their lights on looked safe and snug among the hedges and trees. I thought of a New York City building stripped to the brick, humiliated by sodium streetlights. Why would anyone ever leave this place for that one?

I'm sure it must have all been explained to me long ago. But the reasons why things happen are lost on children. Parents go to great lengths, of course, to make things seem not arbitrary. But who listens? Explanations are very boring and foot-noted, and if there's one thing a child won't tolerate it's a dependent clause.

"You see, Katherine, the sea is made of rain water, which comes from the rivers which are, of course, fed by small mountain streams, which find their source, in turn, in myriad subterranean tributaries, making up what we call the water table—Katherine, do I read *Nancy* comics when you're telling me something?"

So it goes. No doubt that was just what I was doing when the official explanation was given for moving East. Or perhaps I inquired and they said I'd understand better when I was older. I'd have bought that. Since life is really one big dental appointment that someone else has made for you, naturally if a parent wanders up to you and says, "Next week we're moving to New York, isn't that exciting?" you feign excitement, so you shouldn't look stupid, and think, quick, what'll you do with your turtle?

I recall being very discouraged to see that all our possessions fit inside one lousy moving truck but noted, with some interest, that if you turned left past the Webers and drove for six days, you'd be in New York City. So *that's* where it was.

When I told that bully Kyle we were moving East he said, ha-ha, he was going to Catalina that next weekend. Benjie gave me one of his best cars—a tootsie toy ambulance—and Gay Weber baked me a lopsided cake with orange frosting and jam between the layers that was positively nauseating, but custom-made all the same. It was nice to know that someone would take the time, my mother said, scraping it into the garbage. Gay's brother, Cliff, said he'd take care of my turtle and added that he hoped that I wouldn't get stuck-up back East. That was about it. Oh. And Nick Ballard. He sent me a bride doll, and a note, saying I'd love New York City, and that he'd be thinking of me. Ordinarily I would never have been permitted to have such a doll. It was obviously too fragile, too expensive, too grown-up. I'd break it or get it dirty. Never get any real use out of it. The clothes were sewn down so you couldn't dress and undress it. But apart from all these obvious drawbacks, it was also the most perfect doll I'd ever seen. I carried it everywhere with me. I rose to the occasion. I did not break it. I did not get it dirty. I let no one play with it. I resolved never to forget Nick. Not anybody. Not anything. I spent my last night in the West memorizing all my friends and my house. I touched things and kissed the walls. I loved them all. I didn't mean them any harm by leaving. Some day I'd be back. They'd see.

# 7

In those days, the passage from West to East was still fraught with danger. There was the dash across the Mojave Desert before dawn (no one dared cross it in the heat of day. Deposits of parched bones commemorated those who left their cars for help). You could take the northern route or the southern route (I saw a natural live Indian in jeans and a Stetson, asleep on his grazing pony). Roads were washed out, and there were detours that took hungry children and fatigued drivers seventy-five miles out of their way. Duncan Hines called the shots for three thousand miles. One night the recommended hotel in a no-where town was all booked up because there had been an oil strike. Everyone was covered with the stuff. The town was having a party. We tried to order some malteds and a sandwich but everyone was too busy. We slept all in one bed in a rooming house and my mother cried.

Bees got in the car sometimes and menaced the driver. There were Burma Shaves to read and signs promising hokey delights a few miles down the road: Genuine Petri-fied Wood. Mineral Deposits. Caverns. Natural Springs. Fossils. Meteorites. Arrowheads. But like the nice bath-

28

rooms, all these things were usually on the other side of the highway. Or closed for the season. Or relocated. Or just plain reprehensible.

I watched my mother's lacquered nail inch across the road map, her voice warning us to "watch for a road on the right. It isn't marked but it looks like it crosses 101 just as you come out of town. Don't take the first one because it swings south. The second one appears to run north which would put us right . . . etc."

Sitting alone in the back seat, I learned to look for signs of life out the window; in laundry flapping and snapping on a clothesline; a cheesy house with a fantastic swing set; people vacantly waving.

Rows of sprouting crops in dark soil went clicking by. I'd fall asleep in farm land and wake up an hour later in mountains. And my mother would read aloud from scenic guides. Jesse James lived near here. And the Apache. The old Pony Express route. Site of a famous massacre. Gold Rush. Fort Something-or-Other. The Mormon Trek. Mark Twain a pilot on this river. Sinclair Lewis born, right here. Wine country, salad country. Mining. Poverty and cotton. The names on signs had the majesty of an oratorio; Colorado, Shenandoah, Rio Grande, Mississippi, Flagstaff, Amarillo, Gallup, Sedalia, Council Bluffs, Terre Haute. And nonesuch towns claimed the biggest, the smallest, the narrowest, the lowest, civic pride choking in weeds. And diners. A ghost town. "Where? Where? There! There!"

It was a beautiful country, so big its ugliness was inconsequential. And, as its history and landmarks were interpreted to me from the front seat of our car, my mind absorbed something of the past, while my eyes, fascinated, watched a slow-moving combine deal with an endless crop. Nowhere on the horizon was there a home, or a car, or any hope of lunch or companionship for that single farmer doing his job.

When finally I fetched up in the East at a snooty private school for girls, I must have been quite a curiosity. Travel wasn't what it is now. Nobody at school had ever been to California or driven across the United States. No one was much interested in the traveling part, but they all wanted to know about Hollywood. And to oblige them there were certain stories I would tell and, as I told them over and over, I was guilty of making small improvements here and there. The stories got better but they also began to take on a life of their own. To be honest, I couldn't be absolutely sure any more what was real. That wasn't entirely my fault either. Because when you talk about California, it always sounds like you're making it up. And seeing it with your own eyes doesn't help. It even scares some people. Some people feel endangered by orchids at the back door, year-round healthy good looks, perfumed air, the desegregation of indoors and outdoors. In short, they just aren't up to paradise. They rail against it because secretly they fear the jungle will reach across them in the night, tendrils will creep around their bodies, birds will move into their hair, and they will vanish.

I used to tell my friends that I saw Fred Astaire on the street once. In Beverly Hills. Now that was true. But he wasn't actually dancing. Not even sort of dancing. I don't know why he was walking down the street but he was. Maybe he needed a new needle for his phonograph. Maybe Fred Astaire runs out of toothpaste and cigarettes even as you and I (ridiculous). But I managed somehow to leave an impression of that beautiful line holding, yet giving away, tapping feet, a tipped hat, a crooked smile.

Now here's a story: true or false. Betty Grable sat next to my mother at the hairdresser and told Mother to buy Thurber's *Many Moons* for me to read. TRUE. I used to see Betty Grable all the time. FALSE. I just missed seeing her all the time. And Lana Turner. And Clark Gable. Here is how I used to just miss seeing them.

We would be sitting at a table in the Brown Derby (how do you like it so far?) and my mother would say, "if you promise not to stare, there's Betty Grable. Over there. No, not there. *There*. Heading for the door." I'd wheel around like someone had drawn down on me, my parents would hiss at me, and I'd miss her. I was looking for the most beautiful woman in the world and there wouldn't be one. Maybe I expected her to be wearing open-toed shoes and a turban. Certainly her hair would be up, her lips would shimmer, her legs would be showing. I was used to that high-key lighting in musicals and expected that she dined in it as well. At the very last second a normal-looking person in a fur coat whisked out the revolving door like the last bit of dry batter in a mixing bowl. Good-bye forever. Now when I see a celebrity, something inside me rejoices. Hot dog, Don Knotts. I saw him first!

# 8

Oh Ron Wechsler, you of the dainty frock and lightning mind, what have you to do with all this? I turned off the ignition. How the hell did I ever parlay a modest little sidewalk idyll into a book with chapters, and a movie with people all dressed up as me? I found myself dwelling a lot upon that little irony—as if all claims to sanity depended upon it. I turned off the ignition and lights and set the emergency brake so the car would not repair to the ocean below. The moonlight seemed to frost everything in view. Though the light was chill, the air was warm and blowing, a long heated exhale off the desert— a Santa Anna so-called.

I let myself into the house with a key the Foxes had thoughtfully supplied and found them up, sipping coffee in the living room. The lights had been brought low by a dimmer.

As I sat down I realized that I felt very much at home. I told them so.

"I'm glad to see you're doing well," I said, looking around. "You are happy?"

"I am happy," Gene confirmed.

"This is good," I said. We laughed and fell silent. "It's

a good place for kids," I said to Sally. She opened up instantly and started chatting about the schools, how wonderful it was to live in a real neighborhood, the climate, all the things Californians brag about and New Yorkers attribute to bad values. She warily asked me about New York. Did I feel safe there? Was it true that Madison Avenue was lined with street cafés? Wasn't I concerned about the air?

I sorted out my answers carefully. The two cities fight like siblings. You cannot praise one without diminishing the other somehow. They inquire after one another like jilted wives. Though I had spent the greater part of my life in New York, California was my real landscape and deep down I always felt like I was living abroad. And, like an expatriate, I could and did talk about the trouble with home. But the fact was I didn't really like to betray one to the other.

Gradually the conversation modulated to business. Gene and I discussed some of the details of my conversation with Ron.

"I wish you were handling this," I said.

"Ron will make a good deal for you. He's only a little bit repulsive and he's good at his job."

Sally was having trouble staying awake and tried to sneak away, but Gene insisted we all go to sleep. I said I'd turn out the lights behind me.

I wasn't ready for sleep. I felt restless. Hungry. I went into the kitchen and poked around the refrigerator. An avocado was almost what I wanted. I gave up and went back into the living room.

The house was quiet, deliciously so. I had an insane sense of well-being. Maybe it was all the open space, maybe the bed I didn't have to make.

I love other people's things. Their sheets, pencils, toasters, medicine chests, magazines. It all adds up to something done differently than I would do it—proposed solutions to life's common problems. I find myself examining the possibilities. In one home I read *Opera News,* in another, the *Appaloosa News*. Biting into a nectarine for the first time, I say—maybe this will be my favorite fruit. Bring on the health food! A new bronzing gel? Why not? You don't know till you try it. A new packaging idea fills me with hope. It positively makes me happy. I'm middle-class in exactly the ways people worry about.

I wandered over to the record player and picked through some records. Lots of Ella Fitzgerald and show albums. A survey of classical music (someone get hooked by a record club?) and some good rock. Beatles, Joplin, Havens, Doors, Nilsson. Someone must have bought those one by one. I picked an album out blind and put it on. The Goldberg Variations. I could hear Glenn Gould humming fitfully and off pitch as he issued each variation with enormous intensity and edginess. I slowed the record with my finger and lifted it off. Sounds for New York.

I picked again. A Bach chaconne. Musical mathematics. No personalities. The wisdom and beauty of its enlarging theme swept me to its conclusion. The piece ended and the machine shut itself off. I turned out the lights and headed directly for my room. I found my way with my fingertips moving from one pool of moonlight to another. I decided against washing and brushing and combing. Just to keep those sounds alive within me. If you could accommodate those, you might somehow make some harmonious sound of your own.

34

I was nearly asleep when suddenly a memory kindled. Gene had said something to me about telephone messages. I despised myself for intruding upon my own sleep. I switched on the light. One message from Norman Lodeman, the aware producer-director. Another from the airline. Leslie Tyson, an old chum, had returned my call. And Nick Ballard called. My stomach knotted. I got up. I walked around the room a little. Nick Ballard. I'd like to see him. I mean—I'd be curious. But not really. God, I wouldn't like to be disappointed. I'd prefer to remember him. ("What are you—some kind of weirdo?" "Well, being weird doesn't mean you're not nice, you know.") The fact of the matter was I used him in the book. Not as he was, no. How could I? I hadn't seen him in twenty years. But I sort of used what I remembered about him and then elaborated, shamelessly, for my own purposes. He was very glamorous and important in my life once; but what could I have possibly been in his? Still, it's true, when people get older it's not unusual for them to pursue the past, old friendships. He'd been good friends with my parents—though what they had in common, I can't imagine. My father was such a stiff and my mother was such—a mother. Oh God, what if he saw the book? Maybe the Foxes told him about it. "Well, well, little Katie Attwood, all grown up and wrote herself a book. Imagine that. Why, I knew Katie when she was no bigger than *that*." He did, too . . . it was all in the book.

There's a difference between an eyewitness account and the truth—as you see it. Right? A writer observes reality and then works it around until it stands for something. The difference between being an artist, and being crazy, is that the artist forces reality into fantasy, and the crazy forces fantasy upon reality. Don't you just love it? I'll take half a dozen.

Nicholas Ballard must have been—what?—in his early thirties (my age!) when I first met him. He was a lot younger than my parents or their other friends (which instantly recommended him to me). I knew he was famous—but I wasn't exactly sure what that meant. I recognized some of the names in his conversation (Garland, Hayworth, Astaire, Crosby) but since he worked on pictures, and not in them, I was not unreasonably impressed. Now if he'd been the Green Hornet—or Cato even—that would have been a different matter.

Everyone seemed to like Nick. At a party, for instance, I noticed all the men would greet him. The circle around Nick would bulge until it broke away. Women flushed and lit new cigarettes and told him boring anecdotes. I wasn't the only one who thought he was neat.

He was reasonably handsome with brown wavy hair and had a tan when everyone else's was fading. He had very strong-looking arms and a fascinating wristwatch with a big black face and strange luminous calibrations. And on that big face there was a smaller face with a sweep second hand. It could also be used as a stop watch. It was a time factory. When I suggested we get one for Daddy, Mother said musicians needed that sort of thing. Lawyers didn't. Too bad.

Another good thing about Nick was he didn't ask me a lot of stupid questions. I was shy with adults. He let me be. A greeting to a child shouldn't be like a bugle signaling post time at the track.

"Hi, sweetheart," he'd say gently and go right on talking, or listening, or whatever. That was just right. Then after a while he might ask me a question, but the answer would always be easy.

"Been swimming?"

"Not much. Mom says there's too much seaweed."

"Aw, well. What can you do?"

I'd shrug.

We understood one another.

One time when he came to our house, he forgot to bring cigarettes and he took me with him to a drugstore to get some more in his Lincoln Continental. We didn't talk or anything but I felt very important being singled out that way. When we got back, my father blew his top. It seems I didn't tell them I was going along, and he said they didn't know where I was for almost forty minutes, blah, blah, blah. My mother finally stepped in and fixed things up. She liked Nick, and I think she was ashamed of my father's anger. I certainly was. Nick blamed himself, but Daddy held me responsible, naturally. Mother

said that was idiotic. Then the two of them started argu-
ing. Anyway, the main thing was that Mother and Nick
defended me against Daddy which really amazed me. I
was glad Nick liked my mother because she was the pret-
tiest. For an adult.

Sooner or later, it was always time for me to go to bed.
I'd just pray I could slip away without saying good-bye.
Mother was very understanding on those nights when I
just couldn't. I'd creep down the hall toward my room
and hear her say, "Katie was so tired—she asked me to
say good-night for her."

The mention of my name when I was absent thrilled
me. It was like fame. For a few brief moments I could
hear people murmuring things about me. "Growing up
. . . tall like you." "And reading now." "So poised . . .
mind of her own." "She's going to be a dish," I heard Nick
say once. I scrambled for the mirror. How could he tell?
Plain old brown eyes and pale lashes. Freckles. Eeek!
Sugar on my chin. My teeth were awfully large and sort
of drifting apart in front. The only thing that was really
any good about me was my hair just after it got washed.
The boys called me "red." "Auburn," I would insist
haughtily. I bet they didn't even know the word. Ha!

I liked boys okay. Some of my best friends were boys
—like Benjie. But they weren't very nice. They didn't
really like girls. But most of the time, when we were
playing, we forgot who was what. I caught and threw like
a boy, climbed trees, rode a two-wheeler and stuff. But I
didn't play much with them indoors or invite them to my
birthday parties because then they would see my dolls
and floating-bouquets-type wall paper and before you
knew it, they'd start teasing and horsing around.

Now Nick, on the other hand, was what I imagined

boys would be like if they were nice. I really adored him. I remember lying in the dark listening to the grown-up voices volleying and scoring in the distance. And after a while someone would get Nick to sit down at the piano. But it took so *long*. I had to struggle to stay awake or set my mind to go off when the music started.

Then when it began I'd lay so still, so quiet, as if not to startle a bird. If I didn't breathe, it might stay.

I daresay I had a very imperfect understanding of adult life. And Nick didn't help. His music left a mark on you like a bruise. It was all terribly affecting and bewildering. I didn't know the words for it then, but what came through the dark to me then, I know it, was my first real man, passionate and remote. I wanted to grow up.

# 10

After we moved East I never saw Nick again. None of my pen pals ever wrote letters, for that matter, and I never did find out what became of my turtle. Experience swept me on and broke over me, occasionally, like giant rolling waves. Sometimes I was knocked to my knees. Other times I was carried far up onto the beach. I became preoccupied with these tides, studying them closely, long before I tried to write about them. Maybe moving does that to you. Unpacking and unwrapping each of your belongings, finding new places for them. Beginning new friendships, new habits. Unwittingly, one of the many things I brought with me from the West was Nick's tenderness and inscrutability. It had something to do with my own consciousness. I believe thinking about him was a special way of thinking about myself. When I came to write my book, it was natural for me to go back to this first love, if you can call it that. The whole aching business was developed out of a lifetime's fantasy, disappointment, yearning and daydreams. You can *do* that in novels. It's *allowed*. Of course, I thought he was gone from my life forever.

Nick was the first in a series of attachments that

tended to be either impossible or improbable. I developed a taste for love that was difficult or puzzling. I once tried adoring a popular, easy-going, all-American boy type. Everyone cheered me on. I revelled in the approval. We were a swell couple. But, I couldn't make it last over Christmas vacation. It bored me. Necking and breaking off, phone calls, wearing his school ring, getting ready for the big dance. I finally lost him. I tried to get him to surprise me. He just couldn't. He found someone else in five days. She was blonde, with big round breasts, and a neat personality. They married in college.

I didn't mind dating, as far as it went. It just didn't go very far at the time. There were sanctions against everything, of course. Going to bed with someone you cared for seemed to me, on the face of it, a really terrific idea. To enter another person or actually become them in some way—now *there* was danger and excitement.

I sometimes wonder, looking around me now, what it must be like to make love when you're sixteen, when lust attacks you like the cramp. What does it do to people *not* to stop, coupling and uncoupling from algebra right through solid geometry? Hanging on to my virginity was like an unremitting game of "keep away." When I finally surrendered it, as we say, I laughed for two days. It was very haphazard and, of course, meaningless.

Things began to pick up in my twenties. There was a lot more at stake. Careers were started. Nostalgia for one's lost innocence was well under way. Neuroticism blossomed everywhere, like forsythia—the first bright sign of independence. There was a pianist, a writer, a dancer, and a teacher. All were self-absorbed, inattentive, and demanding. Each was incomplete. Quite naturally I hoped I was the missing quantity. It was like blowing into a balloon with a slow leak. I tried to be everything, but it was never enough. I suspect I was not so much in love with these men as I was curious about the intangible thing they were pursuing. We talked about their work a great deal. I didn't know yet that I was pursuing something, too. Or that I was involved in the same struggle they were. I only knew something in them spoke to something in me.

Afraid to speak, I learned to listen and to guess at the meaning of things. My eye and my ear drilled long hours without my knowing. Then, at last, all at once, when I found my voice, I said to the pianist: Chopin is your native language—the Haydn sounds like you're using a phrase dictionary. To the writer I said: Your short stories are overloaded and flatulent—try a novel. To the dancer I said: The work is showing. Give less than 100 percent—it'll be more exciting. The teacher I accused of literary sexual assault. Master Classes in Life. They were sparsely attended.

Listening to Nick, so long ago, I suppose I heard a distant respiration very congenial to my own. In his ballads I heard yearning. I understood about things that were far away, out of reach, nearly yours. What child doesn't? And these things always seemed to be expressed by someone alone—they never seemed to be addressed openly to another.

Growing up, I heard Nick's music all the time in hundreds of places. I heard it in taxis, on records, on TV. I heard it played well and badly. You get used to hearing good music destroyed. A Ballard medley played by two hundred whining violins. A lyric broken up rhythmically by some baritone who knows better. Crooners slip-sliding around a really good melody. Always it would make **me** stop a moment and listen, as if someone were calling my name.

"What was he really like?" I asked my parents one night, watching him pick up an Oscar on the Academy Awards broadcast.

"A charmer," my mother said—perhaps with a little edge.

"That doesn't quite cover it," Father added. Father disapproved of him. He said he was moody, unpredictable, and unreliable. Well, that figured. My father was highly critical of the entire globe for its irresponsibility and unpredictability, all of which added to his increasing and conflicting obligations. This was spiteful of Mankind since he, himself, was a model human being. The kind you'd order from a catalog, if you only could. Considering what a perfect misery it must have been being so goddamned decent in a world full of imperfect beings, life should have been more rewarding for him.

It used to be theorized that all the miseries of the world came from bottling up your feelings. This discovery was followed by the sound of corks popping everywhere. A great festival of feeling took place which lead to permissive child-rearing, demand feeding, progressive education, and a number of other delights. None of this popular wisdom reached my father. As late as 1952 he was still ashamed of his feelings in the grand old sense of the word. Perhaps he didn't have enough of them. It's hard to say. But when one actually slipped past the sentry, you remembered it.

I was playing with Benjie once and Kyle came up and knocked Benjie down and kicked him and called him a lot of stupid names. It was all completely unprovoked. Bullying. Benjie's mother was out on errands at the time, so I took him home with me. As we approached the house I saw Father standing there, watering the lawn.

"Kyle tried to beat up Benjie. And he wasn't doing anything to *him*. That Kyle is the meanest kid. If I knew how to beat him up, boy, would I beat him up," I seethed.

"I thought I told you to stay away from him," my father replied.

"We were just standing on the sidewalk, for Pete's sake. It's a free country—"

"That will do, Katie," Father said sternly.

I took Benjie inside and I sort of washed him up and put band-aids here and there. Then Benjie said he had to go to the bathroom. I waited for him by the front window. I watched Father standing there, motionless, watering his perfect lawn. He never sang or whistled. I was dying to hear him do it sometime, but I didn't dare ask him. Suddenly, Kyle appeared on his bike. He skidded to a stop in front of the house. Father looked at him thoughtfully for a moment, and then soaked him with the hose. It was beautiful. It was heroic. It was fair. It was very funny. Kyle wheeled away, a sodden shadow of himself. I told Benjie what I'd seen, but made him swear he wouldn't say anything.

"Why?" he asked.

"Because it's not the kind of thing Daddy does."

44

**11**

I really intended to call Nick that next day but things got very busy. For one thing, my vitally attractive agent called and asked me to go to a party at Val Murray's that night. That meant I had to go into Beverly Hills and find a dress—I didn't know people were still giving Holly-wood-type parties anymore. And there were all those other calls to return. I'd call Nick first thing the next day.

My sales girl was one of those chicks with so little temperament she never blinked, sheets of long hair, and erased eyebrows. She brought me deep pink evening pa-jamas with a plunge in the front and no back. A narrow girdle of brilliants hung around the hips. Not my style at all. Yet there I was. I scarcely recognized myself. It never occurred to her that I might want something more practical. It never occurred to me that I wanted some-thing so improbable. I bought it.

The shop was dark and funky like a terrarium. Sprayed rubber walls wound around. No right angles. Migraine music throbbed out from a dozen different points. She filled out my Master Charge singing under her breath.

That afternoon I had my hair done and bought a selection of cosmetics which promised to do everything but make the blind see.

Ron picked me up and drove me to Bel Air. He said I looked like the flavor of the month. He was adorable. Yum yum. A whole evening with this bird. He was dressed like a sissy gangster. He offered me a Gauloise from a cigarette case. We stopped for gas. From the window of his Jag we had an unobstructed view of the attendant's kneecaps. We talked business. Everything was going fine. Everyone was getting back to everyone else. There were some changes Lodeman would want, but he and I could talk about that when we met. And if that meeting went well, blah, blah, blah.

One had to marvel at the amount of time people could waste making deals. Cars, clothes, meals, secretaries, limousines. Everyone stalling, evading, cheating, lying, crossing out the boiler plate in standard contracts that gave away everything, adding paragraphs that took everything back. I remember I once tried to read my book contract and found it dealt with international contingencies and skulduggery so remote I sulked for a week. You don't want to read the list of ingredients in a cake mix either.

Val Murray had been a figure in Hollywood for over thirty years. He'd made and lost fortunes (he also took the precaution of marrying one). He was now Rascal Emeritus. Ron called Murray "a pioneer in the Industry." The word pioneer, in this connection, always amuses me. The image of a poke bonnet springs to mind, encircling the countenance of a fight manager.

We rolled up in front of a pair of gates. Ironwork curled around two initials, V and L. Val and Leonora. They looked like something you might order from

Neiman-Marcus. The perfect Christmas gift for *her*. Imported from a manor house in Suffolk. Initials Florentine or Roman. Please indicate.

We crunched down the gravel drive. Someone directed us where to park with a flashlight.

Inside, the house was like a banana split with everything on it. What wasn't flocked or gilded was distressed. Curtains and wallpaper inevitably matched. The living room was all white like Harlow, except for a gooey oil portrait in aquamarine and tea rose of the lady of the house. The study looked like the library at Blenheim—complete with sliding ladder for those out of reach volumes. Everything was leather-bound including scripts. The books came in sets—the complete works of anyone: Tennyson, Bryon, Shakespeare, Darwin, Gibbon, Dickens, Galsworthy, James. All by itself, in its dust jacket, was *The White Tower*.

I wandered into the game room which had been set aside to express the masculine principle: Billiard table, carriage lamps, rack of cues, cuspidor, leather chairs. I felt as if I'd blundered into a *pissoir*. No doubt if I'd had the fortitude to go on, I would have found the feminine room. I like to think it would have been pink and white —a fag evocation of Tricia Nixon.

Where had I seen a house like this before? In Brentwood. Binger. Jacqueline Binger's birthday party. I remember turning up in a clean dress with a Storybook Doll, a popular item of the time. The house was a Tudor mansion with a steep rolling lawn that looked like it had been teased and sprayed. Inside there were a great many adults stirring about. The children were all tarted up in velvet and silk, dodging around the legs of the grownups. I didn't know anyone.

Jacqueline introduced me to her father and mother who were receiving in a sun room filled with plants. Mrs. Binger was reclining on a chaise longue. She wore a burgundy velvet gown and satin high-heeled slippers. She smoked a cigarette held by gold tweezers of some kind. The cigarette was coal black with a gilt tip. She looked quite frail and spoke like an off-duty mezzo. Californians generally speak in simple flat sentences that sound peppy and friendly. That can grow very tiresome, but it was what I was used to. I'd never heard anything like Mrs. Binger before.

"We are so glad you could come, Katherine. Jacqueline was especially eager that you should join us. And now here you are. Do you have any brothers or sisters? Such pretty hair," she said to her husband.

"Nope, I don't," I said, responding to her question.

"Jacqueline has a brand-new brother and is very proud, aren't you darling? Of course you are. Perhaps Mademoiselle will show us all the baby later."

"I've already seen one," I said enthusiastically.

"Have you," she said. "Remember your guests, Jacqueline."

"Run along, adorable girl," her father said. "Isn't she enchanting in that dress?"

"Enchanting," the congregation responded.

"Enchanting," I thought to myself, looking down at my own brown cotton dress. I'd won it for not biting my nails for a week. *Enchanting*. Holy God, I was being brought up in a pig pen. This was more like it.

Well, we had baked Alaska for dessert, just to give you some idea. And if you didn't want that, you could make your own sundaes at the Wil Wright's bar ensconced in a cabaña thing out by the pool, which was lined in delft tiles.

The lights were turned out. The cake was brought in. It was three-tiered. At the top, a midget ballerina did slow pirouettes in one direction, while the cake mechanically rotated in the opposite direction. All this to the strains of a Brahms lullaby—and not the one you think, either. It got to be time to make a wish and blow out the candles.

I looked at Jacqueline. Jacqueline looked at Mademoiselle. Jacqueline seemed to have gone blank.

*"Allons-y!"* Mademoiselle flashed out.

Jackie froze.

"Hey, Jackie," I whispered down the table. "Try for a horse. Wish for a horse."

"I have one," she said sadly.

"Gotta bike?" I asked.

She nodded.

"I guess you've had it," I said. I couldn't think of anything either.

"We will wish for everyone to be happy, yes?" said Mademoiselle, shooting me a withering look. And with that she blew out Jackie's candles. Jackie sat there smiling delicately in case that was what she was expected to do.

Later we were shown *Tom Sawyer*. Right there. In her house. The whole thing. I could not believe my good fortune. When it was all over we came streaming out on to the lawn in front of the house, eyes blinking, jabbering away, waiting for our parents to come pick us up. Mademoiselle stood to one side watching over us all. Each of us had little bags of goodies. Mine included a silver dollar, Double Bubble gum (which was black-marketed at a dollar apiece), Dutch chocolate, and a coronet covered with spangles. Clearly I had had the most glamourous time of my life. I ran over to Jackie to tell her just that. I saw our Hudson pull up at the curb.

"Gotta go," I said. "Hey! I almost forgot to spank you. It was a neat party," I said, giving her eight of the best and a ninth for luck. Mademoiselle swept down the lawn like an enraged gander, flapping and shrieking. "Stop that! Stop that! What are you doing to that child! Don't touch her! What nasty thing is this? Don't you know how to behave?" She embraced Jackie who, in the confusion, burst into tears. I backed off stumbling as I went.

"I didn't mean to. It was her birthday . . . you always get a spanking for your birthday," I explained helplessly.

"No one strikes this child. *Ever*," she said, turning and guiding the child back to the house.

Later, when I guiltily divulged what had happened, my parents explained that no one at the Bingers' was ill, as I had supposed—just very rich.

# 12

Ron's gaze swept across the room at regular intervals like a radar beam. He was drinking margaritas. His amber goggle-shaped glasses, in his case, actually helped him to see.

"What ever became of Vincent Binger?" I asked.

"Binger, Binger—wasn't he head of production somewhere?"

"I really don't know. His daughter was a friend of mine, a long time ago."

"Frank! Over here," Ron said to a short fat man with long hair that needed washing. He wore a fringed vest that swayed like the curtains in a whore house. "Frank Bigelow—Kate Attwood. Kate just flew in from New York. She's got a deal on with Lodeman."

It's weird to hear yourself jammed into a précis like that. We shook hands. He had a selling smile and a confidential manner. He looked directly at my breasts.

"How are you surviving?" he said.

"Not bad," I smiled cheerfully, hoping to divert his gaze.

"I'm flying out tomorrow. On the red eye," he snorted, all but pawing the ground. He got his financing in Holly-

51

wood and practiced his art in the East. He had a fantastic project shaping up, he said, a retelling of *The Canterbury Tales*. Pick up a lot of New York talent cheap. Job in, job out, like the English do. He just about had Stacy Keach nailed. "Fabulous as the Prioress—think about it," he said, his eyes narrowing shrewdly. He was about to continue when a woman with a pale frizzy corona of hair and pernicious anemia came up and gave him a long hug.

"Cora," he said, taking a beat.

"Frank," she said.

"Who's that?" I whispered to Ron.

"Cora Langois. She just got out of the stir. She used to be married to Claude Langois? Anyway, she's written these fantastic songs about why she tried to blow his head off. What courage. . . . Soul."

I nibbled a great many fat pink shrimp and drank two more drinks than I wanted, waiting for dinner. I ran into a wiry little director who spoke fluent hip, although he was over forty, and had eyes in the back of his head. He had a sly smile, wore an elephant hair bracelet, and made you feel like a piece of meat, stamped and inspected. He had a parched look around his faded eyes, as if he had been watching for a very long time for something to move. His conversation with me was surprisingly formal and courtly. I could tell, and was even sorry, that he was really a man's man. I believe he would be called a chauvinist. I found it quite attractive in him.

Finally, after a half dozen more perfunctory conversations and abortive introductions, dinner was served. There can be nothing lonelier, so far as I'm concerned, than being deliberately seated among strangers. On my left was a French director who spoke almost no English at all. I asked him to pass the salt and he said, "Thank you very much." Frank Bigelow was humping him in broken French. "This man, he is the greatest influence in my life," Frank said to the rest of us. The director thanked him very much, and passed him the salt.

The lady on my right, an actress from the Forties who married and gave up her career, told me that it was predicted that California would fall into the sea in our own lifetime. "I bet you're Cancer," she said.

"What?" I said.

"Your sign, dear."

"I don't know—when is Cancer?" I said, stalling.

"June."

"You're right," I said. That was a mistake. She rattled on about my moodiness and practicality, my bondage to the past, attraction to the water. I forgot what she said my sun and moon signs were, but boredom was ascendant. Even Ron looked good to me now.

Waiting for dessert and coffee was like thinking about eternity. My idle gaze fell on my chauvinist director friend. He was staring at me. There was no way of having a conversation—he was too far down the table.

"Cancer," I said, pointing to myself.

"Aquarius," he answered back with a wicked smile.

"Nice to know you," I said, crossing my eyes. He laughed. So did I.

I wouldn't have mentioned all this tedious conversation were it not for the fact that our host, after dinner, insisted that we step into his study and see his new toy. A closed video tape system. He played back the whole dinner party.

"Delightful having you, Miss Attley," Murray said as we departed.

"My pleasure, Mr. Murrow," I said, shaking his hand warmly.

It isn't until after a rotten party you know you spent too much on a dress.

# 13

I really didn't want to make that call to Nick Ballard. Being a writer, I'm an ace procrastinator and especially fortunate, I feel, in being a woman, as there is such a rich choice of activities related to grooming and housekeeping with which I can amuse myself while not doing the thing I'm supposed to be doing. I tidied up some business, wrote some letters, took Annie to Wil Wright's for an ice cream (mocha chip) and dropped her off at a friend's house so Sally wouldn't have to miss her tennis game. I was washing out my underwear and about to take a swim when I realized what I was doing and put a stop to it. This was just stupid. Stifling an impulse to shampoo the carpets and try my hand at paper-hanging, I dialed his number. It rang many times. At least six. I decided to give him two more rings and that was it. No more.

"Ballard residence," a voice announced.

"Oh. Uh, this is—is Mr. Ballard there?"

"Just a moment. Who's calling, please?"

"Uh, Miss Attwood. Katherine Attwood." (What a bunch of made-up names. How about Kate? Katie? You know your own name, don't you?)

"Katherine Attwood?" a voice said.

"Yes," I answered tentatively.

"This is Nicholas Ballard." There was a pause. "Hi, sweetheart. How are you?"

Well, it didn't hurt at all. He really sounded nice. We talked along, in an amiable sort of way, and it seemed to me there was good will on both sides. Maybe he hadn't seen the book. A lot of worrying for nothing.

"I'm sorry I couldn't make it to Sally's the other night. I was all tied up. But let's try to work out something for this week. When would be a good time for you?"

"Well, it's hard to say, really," I said vamping (couldn't we just talk on the phone, shoot the breeze, exchange tasteful cards at Christmas?).

"Sally tells me you're out here to work on a picture. That's just great."

"Well, it's far from settled. These deals fall through so easily," I replied, digging out fast. Wonderful. *I* was telling *him* about the movie business?

"What are you doing tomorrow?" Nick asked.

"Let's see . . . tomorrow. What's tomorrow?"

"Friday."

"Is that right . . . Friday already? I may have to meet with my producer. As a matter of fact, I'm waiting to hear back from him now."

"I've got a better idea: meet with him on Monday. Have lunch with me tomorrow. How about it?" he urged.

I figured there was no point in being rude and I really couldn't think of another excuse. "You're very persuasive and I'm kind of spineless . . ."

"Good. We'll go somewhere nice and celebrate. You name it."

"Maybe you'd better name it. The only place I remember they used to give you Young Tom Turkey and a doily to draw on."

"My God," he laughed, "has it been that long?"

"Twenty years," I answered exactly.

"I'm sorry I asked. Well, that means you've grown up and I've grown old."

"I doubt that," I said fetchingly.

"Tell you what. I'll pick you up around 11 at your place."

"That's not necessary. I can easily drive in."

"No trouble."

"Where do you live?" I asked, quite involuntarily.

"In Bel Air—and I have a place at the beach."

I was trying to form a new picture of him. By imagining Nick I had stopped time. Oddly enough he lived right where I put him.

"I said—where do *you* live?" Nick repeated himself.

"Me? You mean back East?"

"Yes," he said laughing.

"Oh, sorry. Near East End Avenue. Do you know where the Mayor lives?"

"Sure."

"Sort of near there."

"Say—I just had a better idea. Let's take a picnic to the beach. The forecast is good. Do you like the beach?"

"You bet."

"Great. Then it's settled. See you at eleven tomorrow."

We rang off.

I sat motionless. Now I'd done it. That was *not* my plan. Oh, God. What would we talk about? He seemed nice. Damn.

I got up and started walking. Walk, walk. I took a deep breath and let it out slowly, two, three. And in, two, three. I kept walking. Down the cool white hall, one, two. Over the chill green carpet, two, three. Across the sun-baked flagstones and into the pool. Fully dressed. Down in the coolest depths, silent and unseen, I smiled. I followed my lost oxygen to the surface. I parked my watch at poolside and swam twelve lengths of the pool. When I got out, I was weak and happy. The face of my watch had steamed over.

# 14

I didn't tell the Foxes I was going to see Nick for lunch. I should have. He was a friend of theirs as well. But I'm very selfish about certain kinds of encounters and experiences. If I sense they're going to mean something to me, I immediately set about distilling them. Other people are not to be depended upon. They'll talk right through a nocturne, walk right through your fresh snow.

I awoke at six the next morning, neither hungry nor sleepy. It was much too early. I got up and dressed, then went out to the terrace. From where I sat, I could see other people's swimming pools and car ports. Flat modern houses descended in Mediterranean tiers. Early risers had turned on their sprinklers. The odor of sage and mesquite, brewing in the early sun, came bouncing up the canyon. The milkman and bakery truck drove in fast spurts from door to door. A newspaper boy cycled madly, no hands, shying papers at front doors. A dog barked, from habit, somewhere below. And beyond, the immense rigid surface of the Pacific stretching flat from the delicate fringe of surf, curved along the Santa Monica shore. The Atlantic was such a tough, no nonsense kind of ocean, by comparison. Smellier, colder, more brilliant.

We went down there once. At night. I remember it like it was a dream. So close, mind you, it might have been. It was in the book. But what were we doing there? Father would never have approved. A beach supper. Nick would have talked him into it.

Four of us sitting around a beach fire. The sharp edges of personality blurring. You became your voice, not your face. Father tending the fire, keeping the sand out of the food, dividing everything equally. Sizzling meat, fruit, crisp vegetables, wine. A centerfold feast. And real wine glasses for the wine! ("They'll just break, you know. Cut your feet to ribbons.") And a good tablecloth to spread out over the sand. ("Seems a shame to ruin a perfectly good tablecloth.")

I was given a small glass of wine cut with water—my mother's idea. I didn't really like the taste, but didn't say so. I didn't want to hurt her feelings. So I held my glass, pouring out a little on the sand from time to time, and laughed when they laughed. Soon we all blended into a warm circle, like Sambo's butter.

After a while I began to shiver, and Nick gave me his sweater (he wasn't even cold without it!). It was much too large, but warm, and had a good smell. Nick and Mother were trying to remember verses to old songs, and since I couldn't play their game, I crept away. I was full of food, and warm, and immensely satisfied. I ambled along in the dark, no plan in mind, just investigating. The beach scalloped along the edge of the Coast Highway, a series of small coves separated by shoulders of rock. By moonlight the rocks took on bestial shapes, which made running past them twice as noble.

Between the eating and the running, I finally developed a cramp in my side, and had to sit down. I sat for a long while watching the soft, glowing phosphorous tumbling in the waves. I thought about the possibility of a giant wave building out there, even now heading straight for me, an innocent child. I'd ride it as far as I could, and then hang on to the top of a tree somewhere in, oh, Tarzana probably, the wave would be so big.

"I thought that might be you," a voice said.

"You scared me!" I yelped, my heart thumping. I was glad it was Nick.

"They were beginning to worry about you. Were you lost?" he asked.

"I was not," I replied indignantly.

"I didn't think you were," he said, sitting down. "God, look at that water. What a sight."

The waves rumbled in, the spill racing onto dry sand with the coming tide.

"Sometimes I like to be alone," I answered, as if he'd asked.

"So do I," Nick said. "Sometimes. . . ."

"How come the waves are green?" I asked, and he explained. What makes high tide and low tide? And the Milky Way? Questions and answers coupled, one after the other, until it seemed the whole universe was worth knowing about.

"I guess we'd better be getting back," Nick said, standing up at last.

"Aw, too bad."

"Want a carry back?"

"I can do it myself," I said.

We walked a ways and then I stopped. "Nick?"

"What?"

61

"Is our conversation over?"

He laughed. "Well, not forever."

"I didn't mean that," I mumbled.

"I was just teasing," he said kindly, and took my hand inside his larger one. I was so honored and embarrassed all at once, I couldn't speak.

We had to work our way around the outcroppings of rock as the waves slid back into the sea, so considerably had the tide suddenly risen. Then, coming to the last cove before hitting the strand, we found we had been entirely cut off. The water had not only reached the rocks, but had gone round them and was breaking farther in. Flumes of spray shot straight up into the air. The water raced up on to the beach at an angle, and slid back into the sea, taking chunks of beach with it. There was no way around the rocks. And no way up them either, as Nick quickly discovered.

"We'll have to swim."

"*How?*" I asked. Anyone could see how dangerous it would be.

"Hang on," Nick said, grabbed me, and moved quickly into the water. The first wave, a giant dark mound crashed down, pulverizing us, as it broke, in white water. We stumbled and rolled into the trough of the next wave, which curled over us, doing less harm than the first. My arms ached from holding on to Nick, and I knew my weight on him must have been tremendous. The next wave would surely throw us on the rocks. The rising wall of water moved toward us again. I screamed. At that same moment Nick lunged forward into the base of the wave and brought us out the other side, unharmed. The water was perfectly smooth and quiet beyond the surf. I swam free for a few minutes, giving Nick a rest. But I thought of the fishes with double rows of teeth, and octopi, and sharks, and fathoms and fathoms of water beneath me, and called out to Nick.

"Stay near me, *please*, I'm scared."

"Go on your back—rest," Nick panted out. "I'm watching."

"I want to go in," I said, *"now."* I could see our beach fire now, winking in the distance. It was like something that would come to you in your sleep, seeing safety so smug and out of reach. I wanted this part to be over. It was all taking too long.

On our way in, the waves did most of the work. I'd seen surfers cut along under the curl, but when it was my turn, I hit the sand with stinging force, scraping fast across coarse sand and gravel, finally deposited wet and unworthy upon the beach. I coughed and gagged on salt water, spat out sand, trying to call to Nick. He was a few feet away on his hands and knees, trying to get his wind. He crawled over to me and dragged me farther up the sand. We lay on the sand together for a moment, too tired to speak.

As we approached the fire, my legs aching with fatigue, I began to get the shakes. How could I face my father? He wouldn't be glad I was safe. He'd be full of indignation and those stupid lectures about water safety. All I wanted was to be warm, back to normal, home.

At last my parents saw us making our way toward the fire, soaking wet, of course.

"There you are. My God—what happened?" Mother asked, jumping up.

"Nothing much," Nick said very casually. "Caught a wave coming back. That tide's really coming in. Neap tide, probably. August tides run higher than usual, of course," he said chattily, deflecting attention from me.

"Are you sure you're all right?" my father cross-examined.

I nodded slowly. Nick hadn't told the whole truth . . . then what happened to us, it was secret . . .

"You're awfully quiet," my mother said.

"I'm just a little cold," I said, trembling.

"Of course, darling," she said, and threw a blanket around me. Moments later she dug out an extra pair of clothes for me as well. "I just *knew* she'd get wet," Mother said, pleased with her own foresight.

We gathered up our stuff and, after much shaking and folding of sandy blankets and clothes, returned to the cars. I got permission to ride with Nick. My parents took off first and we were to follow.

Nick turned on the ignition, then pressed a button. There was a mechanical humming, and the top of the car lifted and folded into place. The sky was alive with stars. Nick pointed to the Dippers, Orion's Belt, the Seven Sisters, the North Star. He never said a word about what happened down on the beach, so I didn't.

We drove home in a strangling gush of night air, out-witting traffic lights, accelerating on the curves. It was incredible. We drove so fast we reached home before my parents. By the time they rolled up, a prudent five minutes later, we had the car unpacked and were waiting for them, still talking stars.

Before long, adult voices took over again, and I quickly saw that I had been forgotten. It always worked out that way. Everyone was agreeing it had been a great night, lots of fun, even exciting, and certainly something we should do again some time. Yes, Nick had his corkscrew. Yes, Mother had the charcoal starter. Good night. Good night!

"Oh—Kate. I almost forgot. Aren't you going to say 'thank you'?" Mother asked.

Anger and misery twisted together inside. I wouldn't answer.

"Kate? It was really all Nick's idea. Where are your manners?" she chided gently.

"Katie doesn't have to thank me," Nick said quietly when all at once I broke loose, crying, and threw my arms around his waist. And just as quickly, I recoiled. Nick grabbed me as I drew back. *"Katie,"* he said sharply.

"I'm *sorry*," I said, desperately ashamed.

"I *told* you it was late," my father snapped at my mother.

"Once in a while, I can't see that it does any harm . . ."

"Harm? Can't you see she's so punchy she doesn't know what she's doing?" And the argument ran on. And while they argued, Nick held me by the shoulders and spoke, so only I could hear. "You're a brave, strong girl, and I love you very much. Don't ever change. Good night," he said, and let me go. In a moment he was gone.

"All right, young lady, march," my father said, pointing up the path.

I looked at him and didn't move. "Daddy?"

"What is it?" he said sternly.

"Don't talk to me like that," I said and held my ground. I guess I expected I would die for that.

"I think you'd better go inside," he said again.

"I'll go, but after you, because we're standing in that order. And also—I'm not a baby any more."

65

Without a word, he turned and went inside.

Later, when Mother came in to say good night, I told her I hated Nick and never wanted to see him again. Even I was astonished as I said it.

"Shhh," she said, tucking me in. "I don't think you mean that. Get some sleep. You'll feel differently in the morning."

"I feel so—sad inside," I said. "Like crying."

"Then do."

"It doesn't *help*," I said, full of new agony.

"I know," she said, "I know." And she didn't give me anything for it. She threw me a kiss and closed the door.


Well, that was long ago. And what does anyone really remember? A life held together by snapshots and anecdotes. A story told to me by others—and me begging to hear more. Now telling it myself. The great folk tradition of self-deceit. Well, there were four of us, and we did go down to the beach, and I did have a hell of a time. And it made a good story.

The sounds of the household brought me to my senses. Have you ever played that game in which you close your eyes and try to remember what you have on? No cheating? I opened my eyes and tried to remember what I was doing in California. Of course I remembered almost immediately.

Everyone showered and ate. I helped Annie with a jammed zipper. She was off to see a friend. Gene had to be in Hollywood. Sally was going to get her iron fixed and look at some Japanese evergreens out in the valley, have her hair done, take Annie to her riding lesson, recycle the bottles, and I don't know what all else. By 9:30

A.M., the house was empty and quiet again, leaving me feeling like a terrible idler.

The maid was to turn up around ten, but I decided to do the dishes all the same. Sally had such neat appliances. I'd never known a private person with a microwave oven before. And a garbage disposal—those *are* practical. Great heavens, a waste compactor! I filed the dishes in the Kitchenaid and switched it on. It made a fine rotary schlonking sound. I flipped on the garbage disposal and to its thunder was added the higher hum of the ice maker, which whooshed, then expelled its matter unseen. Sentimental even to an ice cube, I opened the freezer and looked at the cubes piling up in unsolicited abundance. I took a few cubes and put them in the ice crusher up on the counter. It was but a moment's work before I was able to switch on the blender as well, the clothes washer, the dryer, the toaster, the oven and the exhaust fan. With the various cycles cutting in and out, the lovely high descant of the blender, a soft muted buzz from the toaster, the menace of the disposal *profundo,* all voices coming together in a wild *stretto,* then concluding with an exquisite, plaintive spin dry (signifying the agony of man), it was a work of substance and promise. Symbolizing, as it did, the random, even absurd quality of existence, its classic modernity referring us ever backwards to the great chamber works of a more gracious age, it was not without a certain plangent poignancy and panchromatic panache. "Funky, futile fun with a socko psycho finish! A Must!"—Christ, *Jerusalem Daily Banner.*

Time was creeping by. There was still an hour to kill before Nick turned up. I was very nervous. I felt like a swimmer shaking out those muscles before the start of the race. I could skim the pool! Except this one had an automatic skimmer. I could read the Los Angeles *Times*! Except it came in seventeen sections and everything was about ecology and how to cook collard greens in fruit juice.

I found an old *TV Guide* and read an article about Rod Serling, his artistic high standards, and the shabbiness of the present market. Right On Rod Baby. The artist was pictured sitting monkishly in his writing room with only the humble tools of his trade: an electric typewriter, a call director, and a digital computer.

I changed my clothes twice but still was dissatisfied. I had to wear my bikini under my slacks and I felt lumpy. Also, my pink lipstick kept going blue on me. And my mascara was clotting. Oh, who cared. Would Rod Serling traffic in such trivialities?

By eleven my energy had peaked and I was beginning to feel plain tired. Then the doorbell rang. I ran to the door, paused, then opened it. There he was. Older and greyer, of course. But how glad I was to see that face. Something inside me buckled at the sound of his voice.

"Hi, sweetheart," he said, grinning and opening his arms wide. We exchanged hugs and I invited him in.

"Hey—you look just like yourself," he said approvingly.

"I am myself."

"You always were," he said easily. "Sally around?"

"No. She's off on what sounds like a personal appearance tour through the greater Los Angeles area."

Nick laughed. "Well, tell her I brought back her racket cover," he said, flinging a pouch marked Wilson T-2000 onto a table.

"So, how are you after twenty years?" he asked, his hands on his hips, looking at me with some amusement.

"About the same," I smiled. "And yourself?"

"Hanging on," he said, shaking his head.

"What's so funny?" I asked.

"Nothing. You remind me a lot of your mother." Nick's expression grew solemn. "She was awfully young—"

"Almost sixty," I corrected him. "Cancer makes you old."

"I was nuts about her. Everyone was. Your dad must have been—"

"They were divorced before she died. I have no idea what he thought. I almost never see him," I said uncomfortably. "He's living in Boston now. I believe he's very content. I get perfectly typed letters now and then telling me technical things about some bonds I have. He sent me my birth certificate recently—" I was getting in too deep. "It was signed by La Guardia—isn't that fun?"

"Aw, Katie," Nick said, looking at the floor. "A lot has happened." He looked up at me with the palest blue eyes, almost light-struck. There seemed to be a great trackless expanse between us.

"We'll never catch up," I said gently.

"No, never," he said. "Well, you're here and that's something." He picked up my canvas bag and we went out to the car. It was a frosted silver Porsche. He opened the door and I got in. He walked around the front of the car. He wore a turtleneck jersey and sweatshirt, old pants, and track shoes. He was very tanned and had that easy physicality of western men. He folded into the car and switched on the ignition. The motor exploded with power. Sitting on the floor (just about) with my legs (long) stretched in front of me (as if for impact) shifting from speeds of forty miles per hour to no miles per hour, and back to forty again, decelerating with gears, wheels holding on curves and down grades (my insides careening and tumbling), everything seemed to drop away. The roaring of the motor dropped an interval, and I realized we had stopped for a light. Also, that my eyes were closed.

"Nice car," I said bravely.

"Want to try it?" he asked, glancing at me.

"No—thanks," I called out over the motor.

"Later," he said, shifting swiftly through the gears. I watched very closely what he was doing, just in case he meant that.

# 15

We sped around curves, swept around normal, peace-loving Chevrolets, and I began to understand the beauty of a fast car. They really are thoroughbreds. The rest are all nags. Fast cars don't mean to make you feel like shit. They just do.

Soon we reached Westwood and wheeled down familiar streets marked with zigzagging dribbles of tar across the surface. The streetlights were as they had been when I was a child, glass globes with little finials on top. "It's the same!" I kept saying, partly because it was remarkable and partly because in New York everything changes. To me it looked as welcome as a turned-down bed.

Up and down and around we went when all at once Nick pulled over to the curb and shut off the motor. I looked at him for an explanation, then out the window again. My house—there it was! Small, modern, non-descript, somewhat dwarfed by an evergreen which had grown, as I had grown, more than I realized.

"It's not as big as I remember it," I said vaguely.

"You were just a little girl then," Nick said.

71

"Proportions change . . . think of that," I mused.

A two-wheeler was parked in the driveway leaning against its kick stand. Printed curtains were drawn across the living room window. I recognized it, all right. But, like an old friend who looks right past you, I sensed it didn't recognize me. I felt wounded. I realized I'd been sitting a long time not saying anything. It couldn't have been very interesting for Nick.

"What do you think?" Nick asked.

"Oh, I don't know," I said, looking away. Yet I had the feeling he wanted to hear the answer. "Actually, I think it's probably the way it was . . . but not the way I recall it . . . you know? It seems very drab and out of style. I thought it was beautiful—we seemed very gay in it, and lucky. Let's go."

At my request, we made a pass at my old grade school. It was a big brick thing with an assortment of outbuildings. Some were built during the war—the rest to accommodate the baby boom. My war. We were the good guys every day, no taking turns. We all helped by bouncing up and down on tin cans, eating oleo, and stripping tin foil off wrappers. On Toby's birthday his mother gave everyone helmet-liners, fake bayonets, rifles and campaign patches. We all agreed it was the finest party ever given and that Toby's mother was the most thoughtful and resourceful and creative person any of us knew. They don't even let you set off your own fireworks any more.

Children were playing in the playground in sand-colored dirt that clung to everything and got in all your cuts. They played tether ball, Annie-Annie-Over, kick-ball, volleyball, and dodgeball. The ground was worn in front of the swings and tether ball from countless years of identical play. I could see the place where I used to eat my lunches from my tin pail. A sandwich in a nice crunchy wax paper bag. A sweating thermos of cold milk. A small plastic container with a mixed green salad inside, soaking in oil and vinegar dressing. A hard-boiled egg with salt and pepper rolled up together. And for dessert, a glorious Hostess cupcake, with chocolate imported from the blue-green-jungles-of-Brazil (or so they said), all moist and misshapen and stuck to its cellophane wrapper. Warm and gooey. Licking off the wrapper was insanely pleasurable. Now they make them so they don't stick any more.

"Enough?" Nick asked.

"I think so," I replied and we headed for Bel Air.

Bel Air is an oasis for the rich. It is uniformly beautiful. The vegetation is thick, lush and well-bred. The houses, like growing things, are spectacular, if unlikely, in their combination—hacienda next to glass prism–next to French chateau–next to Merlin's castle–next to Cotswold cottage—and so on. All of it immaculate and very quiet. A mortal version of paradise. Here everybody lived in June Haver's old house, or next to Buddy Ebsen's old house, you know, over toward Judy Garland's old house, no no, when she was married to Minelli, not Luft. No one ever saw them make the move. Like hermit crabs, they must have moved at night, each shedding a perfectly suitable shelter for a more elegant one, unwittingly left out to air. All living creatures, it seems, have a little side to them.

Los Angeles (throb), land of broken dreams (sob), may be a little weird but at least it's somebody's idea of terrific. That's more than you can say for the Pan Am building which, last time I looked, had wandered into the middle of once-lovely Park Avenue.

We reached the top of a hill and Nick switched off the motor again. We were parked on a muddy plot that had been scraped off the top of a modest mountain. We were looking out over Los Angeles.

"What do you think?" Nick asked. People who live in flat places really get worked up about heights.

"Looks like Los Angeles to me."

"It's a fine view . . ."

"Does this belong to you?" I asked.

He nodded.

"I thought you already had a house."

"I do," he said.

"Do you need another one?"

"Maybe. I can't decide. What do you think?"

"I really couldn't say."

"Sure you could," he prompted.

"Well, I think if I lived out here, I'd rather be down low, tucked into a canyon. When you get up high all you see is everything jammed together, and flat, and ribbons of Freeways, and yellow air. It's like deliberately looking at yourself in a bad light."

"New Yorkers live up high."

"That's different. New York is abstract by this time. There're hardly any trees left to remind you of what's missing. Our best sunsets are made of industrial waste."

Nick laughed and walked over to the edge of the bluff. He waved me over to where he was standing. I picked my way across engraved, muddy tractor tracks. I could see houses clinging to the side of the slope below us. Long sheets of plastic—some a hundred yards long—draped the earth. Nick explained they helped the rain run off.

They looked like giant bandages, which was just what they were.

"Do they still have Japanese gardeners out here?"

"Not so many as before. They were interned during the war. That was before your time, I guess."

"Oh no. I remember. They used to come in their own trucks with their own mowers and clippers. I remember that when they were all done cutting, they'd hose off the drives and sidewalks. I love the smell of water on hot concrete and cut grass. You used to be able to bike through the water fast and make spray."

"I guess you do remember," Nick said, lighting a cigarette.

"Sorry," I said and he laughed. "I really can't help it. All this is more real than anything. I wish I could explain . . . It's a deep-down feeling, coming back. Like catching your breath. A little like falling in love, I think."

"Lucky you," he said simply.

I shrugged.

We got back into the car. "Hey Kate," Nick said gently, "you grew up smart."

"I did?" I said, very complimented.

"You blush," he said, smiling.

"Of course," I muttered.

He wheeled the car backward and then forward in two fast movements. When I was sick in bed I used to run a small car over my knees, down the fold in my blanket, under the sheet, up my shin, at the same gulping speed.

"Where to now?" I called out.

"Down low."

"Can we go a little slower?" I begged.

"You'd hate it," he called out.

"Try it," I replied.

75

He did. He was right. It felt like your first day on roller skates.

"Okay, I give up," I said.

I was hot and hungry. I was informed we were heading for the ocean and lunch.

# 16

We drove quite some distance up the Coast Highway before finding a good spot to stop, a place where there weren't too many people. By the time we found a deserted spot, I was so hungry I wasn't hungry any more.

We staggered down a sand dune that dropped away from the road bearing a picnic basket, blanket, newspaper, and some mail Nick hadn't opened. The waves were rolling in in four straight lines. The farthest line was breaking about a half mile out. The tide was coming in.

The sun was hot and the wind was fresh, carrying a stinging spray of sand close to the ground. We set out the blanket which billowed at first like a spinnaker until we subdued it with stones and shoes at the corners.

I headed down to the water as I always do. Like a strange sniffing dog, I'm inclined to feel you should befriend the ocean after too long an absence. I popped some kelp with my bare heel, picked up a fistful of small shells to peruse, and let the salt air tangle my hair, fill my lungs, dampen my flesh. The surf licked at the cuffs of my white pants.

"Better roll up your slacks," Nick said, coming up behind me. "They dry slowly and you may need them later."

I took the slacks off and threw them up toward our blanket.

"Even better," he said and stripped off his own slacks.

I paused to knot my shirt over my midriff and roll up the sleeves. Nick went on ahead while I arranged myself. He seemed very far away, unknown to me. For a moment I had an unsafe feeling of being alone with a stranger in a strange place. I recognized both people, the man and the woman, as in a dream, not life.

Sometimes I think of the miracle of being able to walk, balanced, on two legs. Or the faithfulness of my own respiration which dutifully carries on without the least assistance from me. I want to fall down. I want to choke. I do not understand where I am or what is to happen. The meaning of things is not clear. And I am a person who likes to understand.

I rushed forward to fall into some rhythm—Nick's rhythm. Walking. He stayed on the hard packed sand. I walked in the water parallel to him, dodging the spill from the breakers. We walked this way for some time. He called to me. I joined him on the hard sand. There was a huge jelly fish—a Man-o'-War. It looked like a sea-going placenta. We stared at it. Nick dug a hole in the sand and prodded the thing into its grave with a piece of driftwood. We covered it up.

"Ever seen anybody stung by one?" he asked. "They look like raw bacon."

I shuddered.

Farther up the beach we came across the carcass of a fish that was tough as a truck tire and all jaw and teeth. No eyes that we could see. "It must have come from very deep," I said.

"Very," Nick said, watching me.

"I get the feeling we're not supposed to see things like that. It's a mistake of some kind . . . look!" I said, pointing up the beach. It was littered with broken timbers, an empty keg, a sneaker, battered shells, chunks of styrofoam, orange peel, all in one place. Sea vomit.

We walked on. The ocean worked on me like alcohol. My anxiety was gone. When the hot sun is on your face, and there is fresh air to gulp, and the suspense of the surf (how long will it curl before it breaks?), you are satisfied. You could probably drop me down anywhere and I would head for the sea with the certainty of a crab. Cancer!

After a while we began to talk. The pounding waves filled in the pauses. Nick spoke in a sort of shorthand. He'd had a bad marriage. He found the world very changed now. Almost unrecognizable. Having been young for so long, he found fifty bewildering. His career, he said, was falling apart.

"But let's not talk about that," he said.

"Why not?"

"Because it's a beautiful day," he said, standing up, "really beautiful. Let's not waste it." He trailed off, gazing at the hazy horizon line.

"But I want to know about the music," I said, smiling at him. "Really."

He turned and looked straight at me. "Are you flirting with me?"

"Are you patronizing me?" I said.

79

"Shit," he said, laughing and shaking his head.

"Okay," he began. "Jimmy Webb I'm not. And I didn't take a lot of fancy music lessons when I was ten so I'm not about to grow a beard and start conducting. I write songs. That's what I like to do. But I'm fifty and the things I care about, well, they won't blow your mind, or cream your jeans, or light your fire—I'm not in step with the times, my dear," he said mockingly.

"That's crap," I said neatly.

"That's crap," he echoed.

"Sure it is. Half my ideas about love, the way you should feel, were formed by those sounds and words. You write the best songs there are, for God's sake. You shouldn't say things against yourself. It's wrong, and it's stupid."

"You're sweet," he said.

"Don't SAY that!" I said a lot louder than I meant to.

Nick turned his back to the wind and shielded his Zippo with his hand. The flame blew out. I helped make the shield with my hands and the cigarette lit. He handed it to me. I took it and inhaled. I could feel where his lips had been. He lit another.

"I'm sorry, Kate. What you said—makes a difference to me. I like the idea of my sounds around you. Sing me a song."

"I'm not a singer."

"I don't care."

"Well, I care. I don't have a pretty voice."

"Neither do I," he said.

"You do, too. I remember."

"I remember something—I taught you to whistle."

"You *did*?"

"Yup. But I never heard you sing."

"Okay. Just once. But if I do, then will you believe that I love your music, think you're great, and—"

"And?"

"And have a really rotten voice?"

"Fair enough," he said, sitting down.

I shifted around on the sand and tried to get comfortable. I sifted some sand through my fist. "I can't do it," I said, starting to giggle.

"Come on," he said.

"I can't make a straight face!" I said, covering my face with my hands. Finally, calmed down, I crouched near him, my arms hugging my legs to keep warm, and sang close to his ear. I sang a ballad of his and he fed me the words when I stumbled. We sat quietly when I finished.

"You see? You do have a nice voice." He got up and brushed the sand off his legs. "Not a bad song, either."

"Not bad at all," I said.

"My turn," he said.

"Good," I said. We began walking while he sang. It was a song of Arlen's. He phrased very slowly—as if he were thinking about what he meant. "It's a new world I see, a new world for me . . ." I walked with my head down. I couldn't look at him. "And that it'll always, always be." As he finished, I spotted our blanket and realized how far we had come.

"Such a beautiful song . . . remember James Mason walked straight into the surf at the end of the picture? I cried—out loud. I could cry now. See?" I said, pointing to my liquid eyes. "Those were the days," I sighed.

"There were days before that, sweetheart. I remember the version with Janet Gaynor."

81

"You *are* old. I'm surprised they let you out at all. Let's eat."

We ran for the blanket. The delights within the hamper were unimaginable. Cold cracked crab. White wine. Peaches, pears and cheese.

"How did you manage all this?" I asked.

He lifted his glass, saluted me, and drained it off in a gulp.

"You always did know how to please me," I said almost inaudibly.

He smiled. "I'm glad to see you."

"I'm glad to see you," I replied.

"Cigarette?"

"No thanks. I don't smoke."

"Sure you do," Nick said, frowning. "Back there. Remember?"

I gasped. "I did?"

He nodded.

"But I gave it up three years ago."

# 17

We ate until everything was gone, including the wine, of course, and we were high and full and completely at ease. So much so I felt I could close my eyes and sleep, safe from surprise waves or critical eyes. My last act was to untie my shirt and pull it down so my back wouldn't burn. Nick tossed a towel across the backs of my legs.

"Not sleepy?" I murmured.

"Maybe," he yawned. "You go ahead."

"Such a nice lunch. Such a nice day," I said, and slept.

I awoke and found the tide had turned and dropped way back from where I had been lying. Nick was gone. I stretched and looked around. It wasn't like me to have fallen so deeply asleep. Way out in the third line of breakers I spotted a swimmer. Nick. I stripped off my shirt and headed down to the water. "Hey, Nick!" I yelled. I waved. He didn't hear me. I watched him swim out to a cresting wave and ride out its possibilities to the very end.

"Nick!" I called out again and waved. He motioned me to join him. I shook my head. I wasn't a surf swimmer. He waved at me again. I took a cautious step forward, I was genuinely frightened of the breakers. Nick dragged his weight against the backwash and came toward me.

"Come on, it's great. You've got to."

"It spooks me. I was rolled under once . . . I think," I said, remembering what I had written.

"I'll be with you. You can't love the ocean and not swim in it."

"Do I have to?"

Nick extended his dripping arm. Tentatively I took his hand and approached. A small wave smacked my bare middle.

"I don't think I like this," I warned him.

"You will," he said.

"I'm not sure this suit's going to make the trip," I said, laughing. It was velour and brief, held together by an understanding between me and three square knots.

"I like it," he said, glancing at me sideways. "This is it!" he said and I did as he did, turning around, and rode the wave in. We were on a big sandbar, so it wasn't as scary as it looked. I got up my nerve and swam out to the next line. A giant glass wall was moving toward me. I dove under it and surfaced in time to see it crash on the beach. It worked! We swam that way for half an hour. I wouldn't go any farther out. The beach seemed too far away. But our last ride in was a long, almost never-ending phrase. It was glorious.

The sun was losing heat and changing the sky to crucible shades of orange and red. My skin felt parched and salty and burnt and chilly and good. I found some boulders and hid behind them to change. I struggled out of my wet suit and put on my slacks and shirt (no bra this time, the thought of straps on a burn was more than I could endure). I brushed my hair and tied a scarf around it. Nick dressed. It was time to go. We started packing up. I shook out the towels slowly, my eye on the plunging sun.

"I hate to see it go," I sighed.

"I know," Nick said. We stood that way, still, watching the day end. The warm colors dissolving into purples and blues. The sand was cooling under our feet. Nick was just a silhouette. But his voice was real enough, and near.

"Hey, Kate. Don't go home yet," he said softly.

"I won't," I said.

He led the way back to the car. Headlights were on as the cars went speeding past. I slid into the front seat while Nick packed the car. We didn't talk. He slammed the trunk shut and folded into the driver's seat. He sat looking straight ahead. I could smell him, or us, sandy and salty all over. As if reaching a conclusion, he flipped on the ignition, U-turned on the highway, and resumed his native, mind-bending speed. We came to a colony of beach houses and turned in. He flicked off the lights, grabbed our stuff, and hurried me along.

"What's this?" I asked.

"Come on," he said impatiently, and opened the front door. He moved ahead in the gloom, switching on lights. Quite clearly, it was his house. It was simply laid out— some big chairs, a piano, some glass, and the sea. I stood warily in the center of the room while Nick moved briskly around the house.

"Make me a drink," he said abruptly, and disappeared.

I was stunned by his sudden rudeness. What happened? Reluctantly I looked around for some glasses. I sloshed some Black Label into two glasses. I'd be damned if I was going to go crunching after the ice. I could hear the shower running. What cheek!

I sat down in a beautiful Saarinen womb chair and leaned into it. I drained off a large amount of Scotch and waited.

Nick returned to the living room wrapped in a terry-cloth robe. He took my drink from my hand and drank what was left. Swell, now I had no drink.

"Really, I must say," I began, but he cut me off.

"Shower if you want," he said nodding to the back of the house. "You got a lot of sun today. Does it hurt?"

I nodded. "Does it look it?"

"You're not wearing a bra now," he said, holding my gaze.

"No, you're right. I'm not. Excuse me," I said, heading for the shower. I wriggled out of my clothes and stood under the spray. I leaned against the tile and let the water beat down on me. I felt heavy and helpless. How to make a transition. How to join things up. How to stop this.

I patted myself dry with a brown towel. Brown eyes and pale lashes I saw in the foggy mirror. I wiped a patch of glass clean. A tan and freckles. My hair was curling along my hair line where the new hair grows in. I wrapped myself in the towel and left the humidity of the bathroom behind me. The bedroom felt cool. I walked noiselessly around Nick's bedroom looking at his things. His beach clothes were tossed across a chair. I picked them up and hung them in the bathroom. The feel of them was illegitimate in my hands. Next to his bed was a clock radio—the kind with numbers that roll over like a tachometer. A tape deck. A Renoir reproduction—an odd picture for a man to have—your standard golden-haired child sitting on the grass. A copy of *Time* two weeks old. An Eames chair. The bed had a fur throw at one end. What to give the man who has everything . . .

"Kate?" Nick called at the door.

"Yes?" I answered tonelessly.

"Are you there?"

"I think so."

"Are you decent?"

"Not very . . . Nick?" I turned around slowly. I knew he was in the room. "Nick?"

"What?" he said.

"I can't think up a question, but I know I have one."

"I know," he said, "I know." He had the answer. He drew me to him now, in fact, just as I had invented, or dreamed, written. With his thumbs he drew my lids down. As I stood before him, he cradled my face in his hands, and the most extraordinary warmth passed from his palms. I could not look at him. I stood on the threshold of everything I knew was impossible. I sensed his face approaching mine. It was terrible. Then soft lips brushed my face all over and his voice repeated, "Oh Kate, sweet Katie. It's all right." He raised my face to his and his mouth came down on mine. For just an instant I saw his eyes shining. I opened my mouth to his and accepted his tongue gratefully. We swept the insides of each other's mouths wanting to know each other at last and all at once. The taste was strange and good, laid down so long ago.

"You're so good, Kate," Nick said, lowering me to the bed. "Just as you are, you are more than I ever imagined —and I have imagined you."

"No. I'm the one who invented you," I said, lacing my fingers with his.

"I'm afraid to touch you," he whispered.

"You know what I'm going to be. You've imagined me. Don't be afraid."

I loosened my towel and showed myself to him.

"How could I know?" he said and was upon me. His frenzy sought me out where I couldn't hide. His passion overtook me so fast, frantically seeking union, finding it, then sighing into familiarity. Desire swelled and broke over us again, then again. I knew of nothing else, thought nothing, wanted nothing.

"We smell the same now," Nick said later.

"I know."

"Everything is in your eyes," he said. "It always was."

"You think you remember me?"

"Yes."

I kissed his face all over. It took me awhile.

"What are you doing?"

"Loving you," I said idly.

"Will it take much longer?"

"It might. Why?"

"I want to talk to you," he said. His mood had changed. I'd missed it. Like a wind that swings around and blows from a new direction.

"Okay," I said and got up. I went into the bathroom and pulled on my slacks. I came back into the bedroom to get my shirt. Nick looked at me and I let him. He put his arm across his face as if he were tired. I finished dressing.

"Hey Kate?" he said.

I went over to him.

"I don't know what to say to you," he said.

"In general—or in particular?" I said.

"May I touch you?" he asked.

88

"You're strange," I said, smiling. He touched me. "Happy?"

"No. You don't make me happy."

"No?"

"Some other feeling," he said.

Nick's kitchen shelves were stocked with an odd assortment of canned food. I managed some hash and soup and coffee. It was hardly elegant but tasted heavenly. Nick took his coffee out on the deck while I washed up. He had soap and a sponge—no little extras. No soap caddies or Teflon sponges. Women are such suckers.

An outside light illuminated the fog rolling in. Through the glass Nick looked different to me. I had to consider him as a separate person. I took my coffee out and joined him.

"Hi," I said.

"Hi," he said back and kissed me on the lips. I took his hand and brought it up under my shirt.

"We are the same people. All that did happen . . ."

"It happened, Kate."

We held hands and waists and wandered around the house. He showed me things, pictures, letters, some shells. It was something to do. Underneath there was something inexpressibly sad about what we were doing.

"We can let go of each other if we want to," I said softly to him. He looked at me and nodded. As if having the same thought at the same time, we began deliberately to exclude each other in little ways. I called the Foxes and made some excuse. Nick finally went through his mail. I washed my hair. He fixed a fire. It was as if by ignoring one another we were testing our viability.

When I came out of the shower with my hair wrapped

89

in a towel, Nick was at the piano. I sat quietly in front of the fire and combed my hair dry with my fingers. He was working on something. He changed keys. He pushed the melody forward a few phrases at a time, making changes as he went along.

"What's that?" I asked.

"Oh, something," he said, smiling part of a smile. He took a quick drag off his cigarette and put it out. He hummed to himself, got up, and turned out a light. He hummed the same thing over again and went back to the piano and tried it, leaning over the keys without sitting down. He memorized it, and turned out the rest of the lights. He poured two drinks and brought one to me.

"You never can tell where you'll get an idea," I said lightly.

He grinned at me. Slowly his smile faded. He shook his head. "What are you doing in my life?"

"I don't know," I said.

He lifted my hair and kissed me on the neck.

The fog rolled in and wrapped the house, and us, in a blind protective batting. We sat out what was left of the evening watching the fire and listening to the muffled impact of the surf outside. I think we must have been charmed. Nothing discordant intruded. No phone or honking horns. In real life a light bulb burns out or you pick up a splinter. Maybe get a sore throat. Something. Not that night. It was written or composed, and not in our time.

In some ways it's the simple things you do by yourself —and are suddenly doing with someone else—that seem the most intimate. The whole business of going to bed with someone to sleep made me feel very self-conscious. Nick gave me a denim shirt for a nightgown. I brushed my teeth with my finger and toothpaste. I borrowed his brush to brush my hair. Nick was already in his pajamas reading a book when I came out. I went over to a bookshelf and picked out a book. *The Leopard.*

We sat reading for a while when I slapped my book down and burst out laughing. "This is ridiculous. Kiss me, you fool!" He did.

"Now read your book," he said.

"I can't," I said.

He turned out the light and reached for me.

"I think soup is one of the best things there is. Shall we make soup some time?" I said, yawning.

"Shhh," he said, and held me in his arms in an embrace so safe I fell instantly asleep.

In the morning I saw that we had come apart, each of us sleeping as we would without the other.

"Hey you: when I'm not paying attention you sleep way over on your side with your back to me," I said.

"I saw you dreaming last night. Your eyelids flutter," he said.

"You saw me?" I said. "Didn't you sleep?"

"I had a cigarette and watched you sleep. I could have touched you then."

"Why didn't you?"

"It's Monday, Kate," Nick said vaguely.

"I know," I said sadly.

# 18

The fog permeated everything. When I dressed my clothes felt rumpled and sour. The house was cold. There wasn't much point in starting a fire. The instant coffee I made tasted like what it was: hot water and powder. Our mood was edgy and dark. It was as if we had awoken as strangers. I tried to make conversation but Nick was uncommunicative. Cordial, you might say, like a stranger standing ahead of you in line. Maybe the barometer dropped too fast. Maybe he wasn't feeling well. Come to think of it, how would I know? I barely knew him.

"Are you okay?" I asked Nick cautiously.

"Yeah, sure," he said, going through a drawer.

"You don't act it."

"I've got to pull some stuff together and lock up. Why don't you have another cup of coffee and I'll call you when I'm done."

"That would be fun," I said, watching him. He didn't seem to hear me. A sense of alarm jolted my system. I went onto auxiliary adrenalin. Something was wrong, not right. I got up, walked out the door, and kept walking, as if I were in danger but shouldn't let on.

The fog was so thick I couldn't see the waves break.

The spill rushed at my feet and I jumped back. I kept walking. As fast as I could. I was stiff and aching from our encounter. What had been between us? "What *was* it, God damn it!" I yelled out loud. No one would hear. A spasm? A natural calamity? Maybe. Fires raged in August. Houses slid off cliffs into the ocean. The earth shook and opened up. People coupled inexplicably and then parted. I picked up a shell. Should I save it? Or throw it away? If I took it back with me, it wouldn't be the same. If I left it, it would be lost to me. Someone had to care.

I sat down on the hard-packed sand and wept angrily into the fog. "You bastard—I really love you. I'm nothing to you, I can tell. I'm not, some stupid, idiot, who can't tell the difference!" I sobbed.

Suddenly, two soaking Labradors came barreling out of the fog, streaking through the water, tearing up the dry sand. They almost knocked me over. They stood in front of me and barked. One stopped and sniffed at me, then lifted his leg and peed on my shoes. "You shit!" I yelled after him. He trotted away, nose down, looking for something else to do.

Shame traveled through my system like a drug. I would have given up everything for him. My name. He could name me something else. I would have lived all my life over again from the beginning for him—if he'd asked. I wanted to bring him flowers and bake bread for him. Read to him all those things I'd underlined. Tell him all the stories that had ever moved me. Play music for him—Couperin maybe, Mahler and Chopin—and in all these indirect ways he could triangulate my position and know me exactly.

I could renounce everything. Agree to anything. How

pitiful and excessive I was in love. How willing to commit the most treasonable acts against my dignity. Doubtless, men despised me for it, believing as they do in survival and thus navigating around the frothy shoals of my exposed emotion.

When I got back to the house, Nick was waiting in the car. He didn't say anything, so I didn't. The fog was piled up against the cliffs along the Coast Highway. When we got up to the top, the fog dropped away. It was a whole other day up there. I blinked as if I'd just come out of a matinee. I was tired.

Nick stopped the car in front of the house and turned silently to me. I reached in my pocket for my key and found a seashell instead. I held it out in my palm.

"See that?" I said.

He nodded.

"That's what's wrong with me," I said, and went into the house.

# 19

Life is so indiscreet. Just at the moment you think you will snap, crystallize like sugar, take on another form, it comes at you belching and farting from all sides. Ron Wechsler called. Where had I been? He'd been trying to get me all weekend.

"My God, Lodeman has been trying to reach you. He wants to talk about the script. I told him you had to fly to Washington?"

"Why Washington?"

"Anyway call him back, will you sweetie, so we can get this mother rolling? I don't like the idea of Lodeman sitting around and thinking too much."

We discussed what I would and would not say in such a meeting and, after a few animal pleasantries, rang off. I tried to reach Lodeman, and after stating what this was in reference to, managed to get myself booked into his busy afternoon. I called Leslie Tyson, my actress friend, found her at home, and made a lunch date with her for one. That put me in striking distance of Lodeman for a four o'clock appointment. I hung up. Despite all my furious activity I was slack with depression. The bright song-bird yellow of the Foxes' guest room was making me frantic. I'd have time to shower and dress. The car needed gas. I needed some things from the pharmacy. I suspected my period was coming on. It figured.

With various little pots of color I improvised another version of myself. A white pants-suit with a long filmy panel, watch, rings, hair up and smooth. I looked chaste, fit, and alert. Very convincing.

Even my car suited me. Big, sensible, cool and quiet. The gears shifted thoughtfully on their own. The conditioned air sifted out cool through the vents. The traffic moved in an orderly fashion. The signs were legible. Every convention—stopping at signs, yielding to the right, slowing at amber lights, helped to heal me. When you lose hold briefly you recognize what a marvelous alternative civilization is.

Funny, isn't it? People ask you, did you sleep well? How come they never ask you if you drove well? That afternoon, I really drove sensationally well. I could have driven to Mexico. Other days I miss exits, I'm in the wrong lane, I just hate it.

I felt myself driving to the music, giving life the slip. I breathed in the smell of the leather. Beautiful. I breathed in again. A light flashed on. The Webers' car . . . the smell of compressed dog. I let my brain just feel its way along. You can read a thought like a dream, if you're quick.

# 20

The Webers were a nice family. They lived down the block from us. The thing I most admired about them was how well they got along with one another. I wished my family was as friendly and out-going as they were. She sewed. He gardened. Their son Cliff was a Cub Scout. Their daughter Gay was a Girl Scout. They went on vacations to such places as Tahoe, Big Bear, Yosemite, Crater Lake, Mt. Baldie and so forth. They had a cocker spaniel named Toto. They had a tank pool out in back of the house which they set up every summer and filled with the garden hose. All the kids from the neighborhood gathered there in the heat waves and Mrs. Weber didn't even care. "Honestly!" she'd declare, and go back to the kitchen and make eight more tuna sandwiches. Now it's true she used Miracle Whip and put chopped pickle in those sandwiches, and that the bread was so gluey you left permanent finger prints in it, but still she *did* it. No little editorials in the pantry about who-do-you-think-I-am, etc.

One day she made pedal pushers for Gay and me. Exactly alike. For nothing. Just to be nice.

"You look just like twins," she said, pleased as punch

they'd turned out so nicely. She was frying a piece of beef liver for the dog. It smelled delicious.

"You kids are growing up so fast I can't believe it. Wayne! Come here and see these two," she called out to her husband. Gay was fat (pleasantly plump) and I was a scrawn (skinny-malinks). Otherwise, or so it pleased her to think, we were twins.

Wayne was about forty, I guess, and worked for Lockheed. He was short and looked like a barber. He wore short-sleeved shirts and had a slight speech impediment that caused him to talk in a mild form of baby talk. He was also very peppy, in the regional manner, and his hair smelled of hair tonic. You could see where his pocket comb had passed through recently. He had freckled hairless arms, he teased and joked a lot, never smoked or drank, never swore. I noted these things one by one and mentioned his exemplary ways to my mother.

"Mormons don't," she said, hunting for a word in her Double-Crostic.

"What?"

"Smoke, drink, or swear."

*"Never?"*

"Nope."

"Why not?"

"They just don't. It's a part of their religion. Of course! Blah, blah-blah, *Hah*! 'Life's but a walking shadow, a poor player that struts and frets his hour upon the stage, and then is heard no more: it is a tale told by an idiot, full of sound and fury, signifying nothing' " she quoted tonelessly, her pencil flying across the page as she filled in the blanks.

"What religion?" I asked.

"What are you talking about?"

"I said what religion are the Webers?"

"Church of the Latter-Day Saints."

"Do they believe in God?"

Every once in a while a child stumbles across a subject that seems to warrant an adult's undivided attention. My mother took off her reading glasses and began to answer my question in full.

"In a manner of speaking they do. They have different Saints than the Catholics, for instance. Their leader was a man named Joseph Smith. He was their Jesus, you might say. And he lived in the 1800s. It's a relatively new religion. He led his people from upper New York state to the great Salt Lake in Utah. That was called the Trek. The Mormons were very persecuted. Like the Jews."

"Who are they?"

"The Jews? Don't you know?"

I shook my head. I really didn't.

"Well, like the Negroes used to be. You know, when they were slaves . . . during the Civil War?" she asked. Still I shook my head.

"Well, the Mexicans, then. You know the Mexicans are badly treated here in California."

"Sure, they live down in Santa Monica, too near the drive-ins, like you said that time."

"Well, yes, but that's not quite what I meant by persecution."

"I didn't think so, 'cause any time they want a hamburger and a malt they walk right over, while poor us has to drive all the way—"

"Kate: persecution means picking on people, leaving them out of things, because of the way they look or talk

99

or think. That's a wrong thing. Did you know all the Japanese gardeners have been put in prison camps just because they are Japanese?"

"I bet I know why," I said shrewdly. "Because we're fighting the Japs and they could be spies or something."

"Who told you that?"

"Nobody. I figured it out all by myself."

"Well, congratulations. That's a very stupid thing to say."

"Are the Webers going to be put in prison?"

"No, the Webers aren't going to be put in prison! Christ! We'd better get you into a decent school before it's too late."

"I was just asking," I said defensively. Mr. Weber would never have said "Christ."

As you can see, this was a very good example of why I spent so much time with the Webers. Mrs. Weber was a cheerful woman and believed in a positive attitude. And, as she often said, she just *loved* children. If you said a cross or catty thing about someone else, she'd say, "Well now, you kids, how do you know she wasn't feeling just right?" Or: "I bet so-and-so is a real good sport most times." That ended it right there. They didn't believe in direct criticism and covered it up like a cat in his box. If they didn't like something, they'd say, "That wasn't a real nice thing to do."

At home when I was wrong, I was *wrong*. Bang! Slam! Next case. There were implications to what I had done, no matter how trivial the deed. Subtle observations were made about my deteriorating character and conduct. If things continued in this fashion there would be Serious Consequences.

While I loved my parents, I sometimes found trying to

please them too hard, so I slipped away. That's what neighborhoods were for. Sometimes me and my friends would just fool around at the Webers since they had the pool and the snacks. Other times we'd hang around Kyle's—he had the best lawn for football. Other times like Fourth of July—they all came to my place. My father was a genius at fireworks. He was full of admonitions about how they'd blow your arm off if you weren't too careful, knew a boy who was blinded for life, terrible burns. Tense and cautious, he'd set off a rocket. There'd be a wild incendiary swooshing as the thing lifted off and for a flash I'd see my father's face, excited and incredulous all at once.

Someone else was the best at Hallowe'en. I forget their name. Poor Hallowe'en. It's been mutilated by do-gooders and faint hearts. When a child comes to my door and shakes a UNICEF canister at me, I lecture him on the trivialization of a great cause: the general spooking and leg-pulling of others. I will give coin to a child only if he assures me it is for personal gain. Let the old bags collect for the needy, in broad daylight.

It was in the dark of night, on the sidewalks of suburbia, beneath an October moon, that goblins and gypsies, great and small, with their oaths and curses conjured an idea so spectacular as to beggar the imagination. It was called the Flaming Bag of Dog-Do. So shall it always be known. One scooped up the ingredient (always available at the Webers) and placed it gingerly in a paper bag. He who had obvious seniority would step forward, ring a doorbell, and light that bag with a match. Then all would hide behind a hedge. The door would open and a startled gentleman, finding a flaming bag on his porch, would do the sensible thing; stamp out the insignificant flames—*at the same time* getting dog-do all over his shoe!

The spectacle was incredibly satisfying and the kind of thing that made Hallowe'en the great spiritual occasion it once was. It was not a great favorite with the adults, needless to say. They shook their fists at the night (so much the better) and said things about the danger of fire and contamination, but we always knew it was just because they felt so stupid. Which was fair enough. We felt awfully stupid a lot of the time. It kind of evened things out, you might say.

Hallowe'en. Mrs. Weber always made costumes for her kids. Gay always went as something beautiful and Cliff was always something conventional like a devil or a pirate. I went once as Minnie Mouse and another time as a left tackle. People laughed at me and ooooed over Gay. I remember once Mr. Weber drove us to a different neighborhood and waited for us in his darkened car. We rang the bell at Ann Dvorak's house but she never came. Shirley Temple's house was surrounded by a great stone wall. Joan Crawford's fence was made of galvanized metal. So back to the car we went.

That car was the only thing about the Webers that I didn't like. I hated their car. It was wartime, and nobody was driving anything too spectacular, but their car was inexcusable. It was too old and had broken upholstery on the inside smelling like old dog. One of the windows had a crack in it and was discolored. It was difficult to start, but everyone thought that was very funny and said it was real cute and shouted encouraging things to it. It occurred to me they all thought they lived on Allen's Alley. Cheering it on, I hoped it would explode and that I would be thrown clear, with Gay, of course. I remember decals on the back window from Carlsbad Caverns and Scottie's Castle and Trees of Mystery.

"Obstructs the driver's view," my father announced when I proposed we might get something of the kind. But mostly I remember a necker's knob on the steering wheel.

"What's a necker's knob?" I asked the Webers one day.

"Ohwowo*wo!*" Wayne said slyly, shifting his eyebrows in an insinuating manner. He winked at his wife. I didn't get it.

"So you can smooch in the front seat while you're driving with your tootsie. Come on Betty Jean," he said to his wife. Betty Jean shushed him. He laughed. She laughed. Everyone laughed. He was a great kidder. I blushed.

"Don't embarrass her, Wayne," Betty Jean warned him.

"Don't your Mommy and your Daddy smooch? I bet they do. A nice-looking woman like your mother . . ."

"*Wayne,*" Betty Jean said.

"Well, sure. She ought to be learning about the birds and the bees. Someone ought to be telling her. They're all developing so fast. The warm climate, they say. Why, in the tropical islands those girls develop at ten. *Ten* years old. Think of that."

"What develops?" I mouthed silently to Gay.

"Later," she said.

At about this time I had fifty percent of everything right and all the rest dead wrong. My teachers were always warning against wild guessing. I sort of got jokes and was making a real effort to understand what my parents said to one another.

103

Needless to say, sex education was bound to be a chore. I once saw some newborn kittens, but I was so dazzled by their newness, and my desire to have one, I guess I never noticed the mother panting in the corner of the box. I accepted the miracle of life as something that was transacted just beyond the limits of my understanding. After all, radios grabbed sound out of the air and transmitted it in a perfectly orderly fashion. Cigarettes plopped out of vendors. Babies came out of hospitals. It was probably one of those excellent technological things.

When we got home Mrs. Weber called my mother and asked if she might show me a book she had bought for her children about how babies were born. I couldn't imagine what that had to do with necker's knobs but the Weber kids seemed excited, so I got excited. The answer was yes. We hopped up and down and and yelled "yea for Mommy!" (I didn't know why exactly) and then Mrs. Weber brought out the book.

It was a pip. Men-stru-ation. Bleeding, actual blood, once a month. Yish! O-va-ry. O-vum. An egg that sticks to the side of the u-ter-ine wall. The *what*? The va-gi-na. The hymen. You had to break it to get in. Oh, no! Often broken through strenuous exercise like horseback riding or field hockey. ("What's that?" "A game, stupid.") Generally broken through penetration. With what? The pe-nis. Help! Tu-mes-cence. Ejaculation. Seminal fluid. 100,000 spermatozoa. Only one joins the egg. All the rest die. Aww. Dot grows into curving line. Line becomes slumping spine with unformed head. Arm and legs like flippers. Fetus. Swimming in belly. Nine months. Belly sticks out like a masterpiece of inflated bubble gum. Breasts hang down like in the National Geographic. Fetus forces way down small channel. Ouch!

Labor. Birth. Spank. Cry. Breath. Cut cord. Mouth to breast. Suck. Life.

I looked around me in astonishment. Mrs. Weber asked me if I had any questions. It was beautiful, she warned me, and nothing to be ashamed of. Ashamed of? I wasn't even sure I believed it yet. I never imagined such a thing in all my born days. I never thought about my insides at all. They just hummed right along. I was hardly ever sick. Now they wanted me to believe that something like a full-length Swan Lake was going on in there. Should I buy that? What if they took it all back later, and pointed at me, and laughed? You couldn't be too careful. But they wouldn't. You could tell from the line drawings it was all true. They used the same kind to show the trade routes in my Social Studies book.

It was at this time that I learned that Gay had just had her first period. I was devastated. Where was mine? What if I had to wait until I was fifteen or something? The Onset of the Menses. It had a noble ring. The Battle of the Bulge. The Invasion of Normandy. The Fall of France. At last I was to participate in a glorious strategic event. Forthwith, I began to treat myself with the respect I felt I deserved. So I was lousy at division. Soon I would be a woman. Ha!

It was arranged that I would spend that night at the Webers' house. We were all really juiced. All for one, one for all. Mrs. Weber made hamburgers on the grill and we all got to eat as much as we wanted, including dessert. We played way past dark and nobody said a word about sweaters or bedtimes or too much noise. We could hear the adults in the kitchen washing up. The light spilled out of the screen door onto the lawn. After a while a car drove into the driveway. Mrs. Weber called out to Gay and Cliff. Their Uncle Ken had dropped by. "Yea for Uncle Ken!" we cheered, whoever he was.

They ran in to say hello and came back with the news that Uncle Ken had brought a whole big bag of marshmallows to roast (my mother preferred those mean-spirited little boxes). Not only that, but Uncle Ken was in uniform. I'd never known a real live soldier before. I'd seen them trying to hitch rides on The Strip, that was all.

We gathered on the patio again and Mr. Weber poked up the coals left over from dinner and we speared marshmallows and browned them. Cliff burnt his on purpose (typical) and ate them off the stick. I tried to get mine perfectly brown all over, but it was taking forever, and the marshmallows were disappearing fast. I finally gave in, burnt them, ate them raw, the works. And I learned there really is a limit to how many you can stand. About nine will do it.

We all sprawled on the redwood furniture. The moon was round and high above us. I was stretched out wrong way to on a deck chair, idly considering the world upside down. The joys of overeating and staying up late had peaked. I was tired and hoping that someone would send us to bed.

But the Webers didn't show any signs of slowing down. Wayne had the hose out and was soaking some begonias. Betty Jean was examining a flower in a tub. I gathered from what she said that it was something very special, like a Venus Fly Trap, only not. A Night Blooming Serious? It sounded impressive. Anyhow, it was supposed to open up one summer night and Betty Jean said it looked like it was on the move. I went over and had a look, but I didn't see anything happening, so I went back

106

and lay down. I knew perfectly well this was probably one of the neatest nights of my life and I was ashamed of myself for not enjoying it more. I yawned.

"You look sleepy," Ken said, sitting down next to me on the chaise. I shifted over.

"Don't," he said. "Plenty of room."

I was still upside down, so I didn't see his face too well. Also it was very dark, and, as I say, late. But he had a handsome voice and his uniform had an unbelievable amount of starch in it. He explained what badges he got —since I asked him.

"Have you ever seen anybody dead?" I asked.

He explained that he had not been overseas yet. I asked him if they were really strict, if he got scared or homesick, stuff like that. He asked me about myself. I gave him the usual answers, I guess. Mostly I was enjoying having someone of my own to talk to, and, of course, the fact that he was so nice. I mean a real soldier talking to an unimportant person like *myself.* He was really friendly. Seeing how tired I was, he stroked my leg and told me to close my eyes. The conversation glided and dipped around us. I heard his voice telling how great it was to be back with the family again, what a swell gal Betty Jean was. Such a nice home she had. Cute kids, too. And Wayne was such a scream. The sound of his voice played on and on without my having to say hardly anything . . . at all . . . whatsoever. The hypnotic hand was advancing, stroke by stroke, up my thigh. The cuff of my shorts was violated. His thumb dipped under my sacred underpants! I sat up like a shot. My flesh was ablaze.

"Look!" Betty Jean said. "What did I tell you? It's opening. Come quick."

In shock, breathless, I stumbled over to the tub and looked at the flower. There it was, a single bloom, all the petals exposing themselves in a slow spasm.

"Kiddos," Wayne said reverently, "these are the most wonderful years of your lives."

I headed quickly, yet quietly (as they always said in the fire drills), for the house and vomited all my marshmallows into the toilet.

We slept that night in a pup tent on the back lawn. In sleeping bags on the ground. I ran a temperature for three days afterward and had a very sore throat. It was something that was going around.

# 21

It would scarcely be worth while paying some central casting analyst type to interpret to me my own misadventures.

"The older man prefigured in the past, *Fraulein*. (Hi, guys! Yawn.) Some early sexual episode perhaps, some suggestion that a peer ("What's a peer?" "A guy in a long curly wig, stupid.") was not deemed an appropriate sexual object. A young playmate perhaps in da latenzy period..."

Yeah, yeah. Well I was never all that latent and his name was Benjie Lindquist—the kid with the parallel parked toosie-toys. He was born late into a marriage between a famous Hollywood camera man and his middle-aged wife. For reasons not altogether clear to me, he called his wife Beauty. Beauty had skin like skim milk which afforded you a clear view of her arterial system and elaborate vascular interchanges. She perfectly fit a description of a person in shock, blue lips and all.

Benjie, her son, was very frail and bony and wheezed a lot, some days more than others. He was absolutely the only person my age who always carried a fresh handkerchief with him in his pocket. I suppose I could be accused of misunderstanding the importance of a detail like that, but because of that neatly folded linen square he had my undying respect and affection. In high school I knew a girl who took notes with a Parker 51 long after ball points had blanketed the field. It was always full of prussian blue ink. It never blotted. Her notes were so beautiful that even now I cannot say enough for them. She could organize everything she heard into heading of Big A, little a, Big 1, little 1. Her outlines decreased like knitting from left to right. She stressed key concepts with a red pencil. One day I was copying her notes (in a sincere effort to become a better scholar) when I noticed a capital letter heading which read: The Hundred Years War. That was all. No sub-headings. Well, such were the losses on a forced march through a syllabus.

Benjie. Benjie was a life-long preemie, you might say. His body was underdone and his life signs were none too hot either. His mother and nurse used to worry most awfully about his lungs and his temperamental digestion. The answer to almost everything was a hot meal at midday—called dinner. ("Then what's supper?" "Dinner, stupid.") I regarded this as very exotic. Lunch for me was a root beer float and maybe a brown sugar sandwich. And sleep was the enemy. I read with a flashlight under the covers or listened to Lux Radio Theater with my hand on the knob just in case the S.S. made a bed check (did you know you could see your bones through the flesh with a light behind?).

Still, I really liked Benjie's weirdness and I greatly admired his lunches, if you really want to know. A little grey hamburger patty on his plate and, next to it, a dozen green peas, and a snowy mound of mashed potatoes. And to his right, a glass of milk with a bent glass straw! Not only that, he had a sterling silver pusher to help him shove the peas on to the spoon (I never could land one with a fork). I guess some people just rated. Moreover, this feast was served on a tray at a child-sized table—a companion piece to his youth bed, which had half sides to keep the beloved sleeping individual from falling out of bed. Those of us who have fallen out of bed can testify to the fact that it's no joke finding yourself on the floor at dawn. It's humiliating, and causes you to feel lonesome and neglected.

Benjie had it knocked. When Benjie chewed he wheezed even more than usual, and his nurse used to sit across from him in her white wedgies monitoring the whole process. It never occurred to anyone to invite me to eat with Benjie. It was regarded as an extraordinary privilege just to watch him eat. And in a way it was. When the meal was over Benjie stripped down to underpants and undershirt and got into his bed for a rest. His mother ghosted in and gave him a kiss, drew the shades, and put a Mozart concerto on Benjie's own private record player. His room was connected by an intercom to the rest of the house, and one could hear his troubled respiration through all its empty rooms.

Judging from his formidable home life, you would think Benjie would have been a dud. This was not the case. He was a fine fellow. He never whined or complained, and we made up really good games. Mother said she thought it was great that I played with Benjie on account of he was such a pathetic-over-protected-little creature. Well, that's all she knew, but I wasn't adverse to picking up a little free praise here and there. I mentioned games. Though it would be naïve to suppose the idea was original with us, we did invent sexual intercourse. While our version was rather primitive and unproductive—and nothing so heady as lust ever really entered into it—it was a nice try. We were not so much committing sexual intercourse as trying to assemble it, you might say, as if it had arrived in the mail knocked down. Tab A into slot B. That sort of thing. But it was no use trying to convince Mrs. Lindquist or Nurse Knudsen of our fundamental empiricism. Besides, I didn't get to those words until much later.

They discovered us in an empty bathtub, and I was banished. I don't think Benjie had any more friends after that for a long time. Every now and then I'd see Benjie and his nurse marching quick time down the street to a swimming pool which existed, oddly enough, all by itself in a landscaped compound. There Benjie would be lowered into the water with all kinds of warnings and admonitions. He would struggle to stay buoyant for a set period of time, and then swim over to the gutter and vomit. Then home again, shivering in his terry cloth robe and rubber shoes.

Years later I met Benjie again, in New York. Remarkably, he had become very strong, with Popeye arms and shoulders mounted on a narrow frame. He laughed easily and talked a lot. He was a concert pianist now. When he wasn't talking, he seemed to be waiting. His fingers drummed out double thirds on the arms of a chair. When he sang to himself he brought in the whole orchestra—woodwinds, strings, brass, his arms conducting madly, the ever-present asthma rattling in his chest. He wasn't satisfied until I was shrieking with laughter. He did impressions of the venerable Madame Lhévinne. We chatted about the careers of Graffman, Browning, sighed over the lost Kappell, marveled at De La Rocha and

Ashkenazy. Our tastes were so similar we found ourselves finishing each other's sentences.

"Katya: I prepare for you a program. You will listen, yes?" he intoned in his best Transylvanian.

His apartment was tiny, but cheerful in a sort of Azuma, Door Store kind of a way. The baby grand was open and took up most of the living room. I sat on the floor amidst forced avocado plants and stacks of acoustical tile, waiting for a cup of coffee which he brewed cowboy style in a saucepan with egg shells. Through an open door I could see that he slept on a mattress on the floor. On the wall near the bed was an expensively framed Chagall. His shelves were crammed with books, many of them French, soft and ragged. I spotted Isak Dinesen, Fromm, Malraux, Salinger, Shakespeare, Cocteau, George Price, Fanny Farmer.

Benjie sat down at the piano and smiled at me nervously. He closed his eyes, breathed deeply—a tense shot from the foul line—and began. Chopin Etude, Opus 10, No. 1 in C major. Merciless thundering arpeggios, chasing up and down the keyboard, exquisite diminuendos, the floor vibrated beneath me. Four on the Richter scale. Benjie's face was transformed, rearranged, as if by a stroke. His mouth lifted on one side, his cheek twitched involuntarily, I did not recognize him. He played *The Maiden and the Nightingale by* De Falla. It's unpardonably Spanish, and touching, and exploitative, and it gets me every time.

Afterward there was nothing to say. We just looked at each other, the music not quite over. We went to a cheap French restaurant and regained our footing. We laughed some more and talked about the old days. Something about him I found very touching. Coming from all those

dark rooms and whispering adults, he'd grown strong
and sat in draughts and ate naughty food and stayed up
too late, and moreover, had discovered a powerful gift
that asked too much of him. I loved him for it and for
making sense to me now, after all the dreadful discon-
tinuity of growing up.

I recall a candle sweating between us while we waited
for our *café filtre*. I chased bread crumbs across the table
cloth with a moistened finger. A little battered coffee pot
arrived along with two cups and saucers. The coffee
wasn't ready yet. His cigarette trembled between his fingers. He told me that his mother had told him that if he
ever touched a girl again after me, his penis would fall off.
She undoubtedly spoke from conviction, because he believed her, and had taken the precaution of becoming a
homosexual. He had been in analysis eight years. I listened
silently but my face stung. He was paying me the com-
pliment of perspective and compassion. I would understand. I was that sensitive.

I carefully dodged any moral responsibility for ruining
his life. All of social science had seen to that. Still, it felt
like homicide, and I could see myself as an accessory to
the crime. The bastard! I had my grievances too. For all
my inadequacies as a courtesan, I had, after all, loved
him—asthma, mashed potatoes, and all. His sudden leaving when we were children introduced me to the notion
that a man could love you with his body, and not love you
at all. Leave. *That* fear was prophetic, whereas everyone
knows your penis won't fall off, no matter how gothic
Mama's motivation.

Odd, how driving induces thought. You've left but you
haven't arrived yet. It's like weighing yourself. In my
tremulous state of imbalance I accused myself of consort-

ing with the past and having carnal knowledge of my own memories (that ought to be worth five to ten in the Danbury Pen—all the nicest people go there. The Water Commissioner, the Berrigan brothers . . .) Had I anything to say in my own defense?

I always have something to say in my own defense. I find nostalgia a deep, perhaps even sexual, response to first impressions. Through it we cherish our innocence and also a certain fluttering of the eyelids signifying consciousness. There must be a first time you get drunk on wisteria or see real color, radiant and unexpected—and you understand what blue can be. Some time, somewhere, you touch something and instead of moving it, it moves you. All these are primary hypnotic suggestions that work on you all your life. And with nostalgia comes forgiveness. I could forget the calamity with Benjie. It was his friendship and the wonderful long afternoons we spent together, not fighting, that I remembered now. And I could forget the soldier's midnight grope and all the sophisticated things I had come to think about the Webers, and remember, instead, that certain sun-burned feelings of well-being we shared together.

In time wouldn't I remember Nick the same way? Yes, of course. I would think of him on the beach, separate from me, walking ahead. See, I cheat a little, knowing how it all works. I make things to remember, so I'll never run out.

# 22

Leslie Tyson and I had gone to college together. She was one of those people who knew how things worked. How to stop a check, where to get an abortion, what a dollar was worth in pounds sterling—that kind of thing. She could get tough when she had to, and the words came to her. But she couldn't get the top off a pickle jar. She was a disarming combination of strength and weakness that both charmed and infuriated me. We were solid friends and respected each other's judgment somehow, despite the usual deficiency of same on both sides. But when we were in college, girls didn't have much judgment—it simply wasn't encouraged. Ooops they were pregnant, ooops they were broke. Few of them really did any work, or gave a damn about anything. But Leslie did—and I did, I guess. So we were friends. Her decision to become an actress was one of those things I never understood. Acting seemed to me a second-rate enterprise, for girls who didn't, or couldn't, finish their sentences. She told me I was full of shit. Good old Leslie.

Leslie lived in a scratchy stucco apartment building on an uphill street above The Strip. The address ran to four numbers and a fraction.

"Up here," a familiar voice called out. A small outside staircase ran up to the apartment on the second level. Leslie held the screen door open with her hip and held a small white dog in her arms.

"How are ya, babe?" she said, smiling. Most of her face was hidden behind one-way sunglasses.

"Okay," I said, giving her a kiss on the cheek. Leslie was wearing a leotard and jeans and a large soft shoulder bag.

"I just got back from class, hope I don't stink. Meet Ivan," she said, holding out her dog.

"The Terrible?" I asked, patting his head.

"Terrible doesn't begin to cover it. He ate my wallet last night—didn't you?" she said, kissing him and tossing him indoors. "So: welcome to sunny California. You look good. Prosperous, chic, very New York. Nice suit. How are you?"

"I feel like a leper, to be perfectly honest."

"Terrific. We'll have a long, extremely personal conversation—as soon as I have a shower. Have some coffee?"

"No thanks."

"I'll only be a minute. Have a look around. There are some figs in the fridge," she added, then disappeared.

I sat by myself for a moment doing nothing—listening to the shower, annoyed to be sitting there all alone. For just a moment I was mad at Leslie, but I got over it. Still, there is something about actors . . . they have a way of upstaging you with a phone call, or impersonating themselves instead of being themselves, at the moment you need them. Instead of being sad, they "do" sad. Laughter becomes a silvery tinkle, anger causes them to pace. They syncopate their phrasing to show emotion and thought. Well, it's *true*. Still, Leslie scarcely deserved all this resentment. I pulled myself together and got a fig. I pulled back the wrinkled purple skin and ate the seeded dark rose meat. How anything so repulsive looking can be so delicious is beyond me. The fig restored my good spirits.

Leslie's apartment, I discovered upon inspection, was like her room at college. A mess. It made me laugh. It was a nice mess, full of thought not quite carried out. Some big paper flowers were stuffed into a jug on the floor. A cast-off couch—a Late Heavy Litter Night period piece—was improved if not redeemed, by bright pillows. Trade papers and opened mail were strewn across a low marble table. A script with pencilled cuts lay open on the floor. Leslie came back through the living room in various states of undress, muttering apologies, retrieving towels from a closet, soap from the kitchen, her purse from the bedroom.

It occurred to me, watching her move back and forth, that my whole relationship with Leslie was one long conversation that life kept interrupting. We could almost always pick up where we left off. We had our differences (we always gave each other the wrong Christmas presents) but if it came to a kidney transplant, I knew she'd be there.

"Oh, that's better," Leslie said, sinking into a chair, her hair twisted in a towel turban. Her eyebrows were no longer sketched in, and she wasn't wearing her eyelashes. Her skin was very pale.

"How come you don't look healthy?" I asked.

"Does everybody have to look healthy?"

"You're the only person I've seen in five days who doesn't have a tan."

"I'm nursing my pallor. I stay out of the sun. It's the only way I can be sure I'm who I think I am."

"Who's that?"

"I forget. No, actually I'm about forty-three, I think, dying of a wasting disease . . ."

"Which one?"

"Time, my dear, time. There's no work. And what there is is so lousy. I've played one policewoman, a crazed southern deb," she ruefully counted the roles on her fingers, "an oceanographer who talks to porpoises, and a junkie. The porpoises weren't bad, but the scripts are unbelievable. I seem to spend my life repeating words no one ever said. Looking for motivation where there is none." Leslie cleaned the lenses of her glasses on her shirt tail, peered through them, and put them back on. "I just came off a show—your sickle cell anemia plot. The attending physician was our hero, a funky M.D. who rides a hog to work. Vroom, vroom. You bet. When he's not wearing his custom-fitted doctor suit, he wears a jumpsuit and Gucci loafers. They filmed it in Watts to give it that sting of reality. Who writes those things, anyway? Why don't you write something for TV?"

"As a matter of fact I'm out here to talk to a guy about turning my novel into a screenplay."

"Who's that?"

"Norman Lodeman. Ever hear of him?"

"*That* asshole. Oh, well, good luck."

"Is he really terrible?" I asked, not wanting to know the answer.

"Well, they're all terrible. It just depends on which one you're discussing. Lodeman is—let's see, sort of deliberately groovy. Know what I mean?"

"Yes," I sighed.

119

"He and his wife went to Esalen or some damn thing . . . they claim to have encountered something. I can't imagine what . . . apparently they sat naked together in a warm pool of water and it changed their lives," she shrugged.

"Have you ever worked for him?"

"No—I know his wife. She sometimes takes class with me."

"What kind of class?"

"A sort of all-purpose Yoga-Aikido thing. Anyhow, she takes deep breathing very seriously. The teacher talks like Bela Lugosi—she stalks around saying, 'Our bret is da life force. We are forcing all tauts from our consciousness . . . Soon we are leeequifying . . . our balance is like two stones softly rolling between our ears . . . ahhh laavly,' she says, and we turn around and Dingaling is in a trance. Gone. We had to call the Fire Department."

We conducted a brief assault on the refrigerator and moved out onto a small, warping porch. Leslie sat under an umbrella while I sat in the sun. We ate plain tuna out of the can, with lemon juice and Worcestershire sauce, cottage cheese, and cantaloupe slices.

"I was starved," I said, filling in a long chewing silence. Food in the stomach and sun on my head and shoulders. I felt myself softening up a bit. I had a funny feeling I was going to ask Leslie about Nick.

"Remember Mindy Stewart?" Leslie asked.

"Sure," I said. Mindy was a suite-mate of ours in college. "I heard she got married."

"*Married*. Divorced!"

"That was quick."

"Something about voyeurism, I think. That doesn't

120

sound right, does it? Nobody peeks any more. It must have been impotence."

"That doesn't sound right, either. Everybody swings. Have you ever met a guy that didn't?"

"Nope."

"Me either. See? It's like all those statistics that say 93 percent of all Americans believe in God. I don't know one. Do you?"

"Nope," Leslie said, picking up our plates and taking them into the kitchen.

"I saw Joan and Mort in Boston—I was up there promoting the book," I called out to her. She came back through the screen door. When was I going to ask her about Nick? Joan and Mort. After them.

"How are they?" Leslie asked.

"Okay, I think. Remember what a fantastic brain she was? She used to run her academic life like a small business. Up at seven. Breakfast in the dining room. There were only about six people who ever turned up for breakfast. In the library by 8:30. She taught herself German with Berlitz records. Remember? She knew how to touch type . . . well, now she has four boys about nine months apart, and varicose veins. Her house is a shambles. I mean *broken*. Her kids are completely wild. I saw one of them eat a whole loaf of bread! They drink a lot of Gallo wine and have his students in for meals. I wanted to send them a rug when I was in Spain, but I was afraid they'd hang it on the wall. Anyhow, she is absolutely content. Figure it out."

"When I see what you have to do to be content I sometimes think I may never make it," Leslie sighed.

"Oh, I don't know. I suppose you could do worse than go into business raising human beings."

"I don't know if I like kids."

"*No?*"

"Mmmm, I think I like them until I get with them. They never want to do what I want to do. I mean adults and kids really have nothing in common. Also, I guess I'm a little nervous for them. Being a child is such a nightmare."

"Do you really think so?"

"I *know* so," she said, field-stripping her cigarette.

"Didn't you like being a child?"

"I hated it. I was a lousy child. I had terrible parents —they were okay as people and all. We were just a flop family."

"I don't believe that," I scolded her.

"You ought to. When Daddy was hot in the business, the kids wouldn't play with me because they figured I was stuck up. We were living in Beverly Hills. Then when he was blacklisted, the kids wouldn't play with me because they figured I was a Communist. Like it would get *on* them. Guys in business suits used to sit in cars and watch the house. The phone was tapped. We used to get on the phone and say, 'Hi, everybody.' There really were bogey men when I was little. I saw them."

"But not really really."

"Yes, really really."

Why is it that the truth is always negative? Or was it just that everything negative tended to sound like the truth? Leslie was absolutely sure about everything. I hesitated before submitting anything so ambiguous as my own life to her, but I chanced it.

"What do you know about Nicholas Ballard?" I asked, feigning indifference.

Leslie smiled at me (she knew me too well) then frowned.

"Nicholas Ballard. He goes back a long way. My parents used to know him. He went to the same parties, that kind of thing. I don't know much about him, come to think of it. I don't think anybody did. He's still alive, I know that. Very private—never any publicity. Why?"

"Just curious," I said.

"Just curious," she repeated. She gazed at me patiently. Her sunglasses threw back a fun house image of me in my chair. "Does he mean something to you?"

"I'm afraid so, but I don't know what I'm going to do about it."

"Are you having an affair?"

"What a delightful way to put it. No, nothing so substantial. It was more like—a viral infection. Lasted about forty-eight hours . . ."

". . . Up and around in no time," Leslie added. "We've had this argument before but *really*, this is a no-good place. It's the crazy way things grow. It's emotionally tropical, too. Things grow very fast, and big, and die. It doesn't just rain out here, you know. First there's no rain. Then suddenly there is rain. A lady I know was getting out of her car, stepped into the gutter accidentally, was swept off her feet, dragged under the car, and drowned. Just like that." Leslie stopped abruptly. A bee was menacing her. She told him to buzz off and sat down again. The bee was back again, hovered, then settled on her arm.

"Shit! Now what do I do?"

"Be still—he'll go away. Go on—you were saying . . ."

123

"The people," she said, edgily watching the bee browse through the blonde hairs on her arm, "there are so many people . . . who've had all they're going to have . . . they're still around . . . shit, I really think he's going to sting me, Kate."

"He's not going to sting you," I said firmly.

She grimaced and picked up where she left off. "Anyhow, those people are dangerous. They keep practicing their serve, putting together Mickey Mouse business deals, declaring bankruptcy, staging comebacks. You see them turn up on the talk shows and someone like David Frost asks them what their definition of love is, and then toodledoo. There's something about them that's very brave and touching, and they'd eat you for breakfast. Most of them yak about the new morality, or lack of it. One dame I know was complaining about frontal nudity. Thirty years ago there wasn't a director in town who hadn't seen her frontals at one time or another."

The bee was airborne again and we watched it swoop erratically over a leftover lump of cottage cheese.

"I know what you're saying, but I still like it here. It's improvised, and funny, and still beautiful. To me. And people, what the hell, they're all dangerous. So back east they read *The New York Review*. So what?"

"At least they can read."

"I wouldn't attach too much importance to that."

"You're anti-intellectual."

"You bet. I'm opening a chain of nutburger stands," I said.

"The bee's on you now." Leslie smiled and pointed at my leg.

"*Where?*" I said, sitting up fast. "*Now* what? Christ, I hate those things."

124

"Theorist!"

"It was different when he was on you. He didn't really have his mind on what he was doing. Look at him now. He looks irritable."

"I'm sure if you just forget about him, he'll go away. What's Ballard like?"

"Oh, *really*, with a bee on me?"

She smiled an evil smile.

"Well," I said, "as you so adroitly put it, he's still alive." Knowing the bee might sting me, and even die because of it, troubled me more than it should have. Why should either of us get hurt? "I love him, I know that. But I think it's not a good idea to get too close to him."

"What are you to him?"

"I wish I knew. I'll have to figure that out some time. The simplest answer is unacceptable to me. I thought I'd work on something more complicated—and flattering."

"Of *course*." Leslie said. "Say girls! Want to make big money in your spare time? Take our thirty-day crash course in self-delusion! Impress your boss! Make new friends! If not completely satisfied, return to us, postage free, the unused portion of your life—"

"Oh, stop doing Eve Arden," I said irritably.

"Look, it's a matter of the greatest indifference to me, Kate, what you do. I mean, Ballard I don't know. He could wake up dead in bed tomorrow and all I could say would be, 'Yeah, I knew someone who knew him,' and whistle a few bars of "This Time." You I don't see any more. So I figure it's none of my business—"

"Shut up and listen. I care very much for him. And about him. He's one of those people. He affects me. Do you understand?"

"I guess so."

125

"Someone you know for a long time and like—you say you love them, don't you? I mean it's not too much to say. Right?"

"I guess not. No."

"Okay. I knew him a long time ago. Then when I saw him again—I was too glad to see him. But I didn't think about it. I must have come on like a truck. I can't bear what he must think of me."

"Oh, *really* Kate. Who cares? And how about him? Some old has-been picking off young lovelies—"

"It wasn't *like* that. I turned him on."

"I still say he's no hero."

"I miss him," I said to Leslie.

"You think it's over?"

"I'm sure of it," I said.

"Well, it's a goddamned shame," Leslie said frowning. "At the risk of changing the subject—may I suggest we run like hell?"

We did. Into the house with the screen door banging. But not fast enough. We found it takes two college graduates about eight minutes to get a stinger out. Leslie called downstairs and asked the neighbors what you do for bee stings. Cold mud, they said. So we made cold mud. We packed it on my forearm. The stinging gave me the shivers.

"Well, here I go. Off to make my fortune—with a broken heart and mud on my arm."

"Aren't you glad you took algebra and two years of Latin? Such a help in later life," Leslie laughed and waved at me. I liked her.

# 23

Just to begin with, Norman Lodeman had the best look-ing secretary I ever did see. Moreover, she seemed to do nothing secretarial. She was English and thin. Such breasts as she had were ingenuously displayed through a shirred gauze blouse. For a skirt she wore a hank of split rawhide and lavender Scaramouche boots. She moved restlessly about the outer office like a visiting niece. She dallied with the Call Director, adjusted the stereo and the thermostat on the air conditioner. There was a piece of paper in her orange electric typewriter. She sat down to type. She punched on the dictating machine. Her little rosebud mouth formed a silent question. Her astonishing eyelashes fluttered a moment, and she switched it off again. Not today. She freshened her lipstick and took a paperback out of her desk drawer. A baby spotlight pin-pointed a vase of sweetheart roses on her desk. She moved the vase and maneuvered her book at arms' length into the light. Like so many people of negligible intelligence, she read long books.

"*Papillon*," she said, holding the book up. "Marvelous —ever read it?"

"No," I said.

"Absolutely super," she said.

"Yes?"

"Hmm. Care for a yogurt?"

"No thanks."

She disappeared and returned with a bowl of yogurt. She sat contentedly spooning the stuff into her mouth and reading. Looking around, I was struck by how much of a home an office is. Furniture, carpeting, plants, food, TV, stereo. On the wall there was a Dubuffet of the Queensboro Bridge, presumably to remind us that Lodeman began in New York.

The door to the inner office opened and a man stuck his head out.

"Shirley, get Lou Kelly on the phone. And call the phone company and have them send someone over to fix the fucking interoffice phone, will you? This is ridiculous. Oh, and cancel lunch tomorrow with Tom. Tell him I have *herpes simplex* or something. We'll get back to him. Kate Attwood?" he said, looking at me.

"Yes," I said.

"I'm all jammed up in here—I've got a call into Dusseldorf—five minutes, that's all. Make yourself comfortable. Get Miss Attwood some Crunchy Granola or something, huh, Shirl?" he called out then shut the door.

Twenty-five minutes later I was seated in the inner office across from Lodeman. He was still on the phone but nodded to a chair across the desk from him. I sat down. He spun around in his chair, turning his back to me, and pressed his index finger against his spare ear.

Well, I thought to myself, I've lived my whole life, sat long hours trying to figure it all out, written it up, and here I am. Looking at the thinning hair of a man who could not possibly know how little I like him already, yet

128

alleges to love my work. How could he? He wheeled around, made a notation on a pad, and hung up.

"Shirley!" he yelled. "No calls. I'm in conference. How about something to eat?" he said, slapping his palms down on the desk.

"Nothing for me. Thanks."

"Shirley! Bring in that menu. Great deli two blocks from here. Better than the Stage. Get me a sturgeon on pumpernickel, Harp beer, and figs for dessert. How about you?"

"No, really, I've eaten."

"Shirley! Order Miss Attwood the summer borscht. You don't like it, you don't have to eat it. Just try it. Made fresh every day."

"So," he said, rubbing his hands together, "this your first trip out here?"

"No," I said, my voice wavering a little. "The book— it was about California."

"That's right—you were a kid here or something. Where are you staying?"

"With friends," I said.

"Right," he replied, thinking about something else. "Shirl! Make that rhubarb! No figs!"

He wrung his hands and paced the floor—the very picture of fierce concentration. It occurred to me he might be trying to remember who I was and what I was doing there. "So, now, down to cases, let's see. The book. Let me say right up front: it's a fantastic book. Very moving, very moving. Shirl! Get me the file on Miss Attwood," he bellowed again. "I made some notes I wanted to go over with you, get your reactions. Keep everything organized. Better that way. Tell me: how do you like L.A.?"

"I like it very much."

"Been over to see the Museum of Art?"

"I drove by it."

"Would you believe that used to be a garbage dump? I love irony."

"A tar pit."

His brows stitched together for an instant.

"It isn't entirely an irony," I plodded on. "That is to say, it used to be full of old bones. Mastodons and stuff. Relics from the past. It still is. So to speak. Actually it's more of a garbage dump," I conceded at last.

"They have a lot of fabulous paintings in there."

I nodded ambiguously.

"But of course we New Yorkers are used to the very best."

The sturgeon and borscht arrived just in time to save us from ourselves. Shirley took everything out of paper bags and distributed the contents on to china plates and bowls.

"Genuine Spode," Lodeman said, picking a slice of bermuda onion out of his lap. "Now here's the deal— don't let me rush you through your soup—you want some tea? Oolong? Orange pekoe? Darjeeling?"

"No, thanks, really," I pleaded.

"Mint tea—it's an ancient remedy—"

"I really don't have anything wrong with me."

"Right," Lodeman said, already thinking about something else. "A lot of guys I know, they buy something, they think they own it. I don't work that way. Right?"

"Right," I said. Now he had me doing it.

"I understand what it is to be a creative person and I think producers and directors and writers should work

130

harmoniously. They are what we call a meaningful unit when the lines of communication are open. *Right?*"

I wouldn't say it, but it was like suppressing a hiccup.

"What I'd like to do, Miss Attwood—Kate?—is talk through the story with you so we can get a gut understanding of our creative intentions. Then I'll tell you how to fix it up. That way we understand each other. Right? Right. Going from a book to a screenplay entails certain mutations—notice I didn't say mutilations—mutations."

He took a dramatic pause and began afresh. "Forget everything I just said. Suppose you tell me what you think this book is about," he said, tipping his chair backwards and closing his eyes.

I hadn't given a book report since eighth grade, and I had that terrible sinking feeling that I wasn't prepared. Except I wrote this one. Christ, what was it about? "You want a summary?"

"Shoot," he said.

"The theme . . . the *thrust* . . . is the invalidation of sentimentalism."

Lodeman's eyes popped open like a snoozing Doberman. "I like that," he said guardedly. "Go on."

It did have sort of an authentic ring to it. All that fancy Eastern schooling has its uses.

"We abridge the past to suit ourselves. The past rises up—threatens the present—continuity is threatened. Our lives are built on a misunderstanding of the past, you might say."

"So basically, what we have here is a modern love story," Lodeman said and began pacing again.

He peeked between the slats in his venetian blinds.

131

"We are dealing with an audience that was born in the Fifties. I think the late Forties are going to be very big now. We've seen the Thirties and the early Forties. This is a chance to do the late Forties. A period piece. A costume picture, if you will, without costumes. It could have a nice look. Skirts down to here. The kids would like that. I like to think that as film makers, we're putting a whole generation in touch with its past. We have a responsibility beyond entertainment: to educate. I often speak to groups of film students—they pay rotten but they're very talented and dedicated. Last week I was talking to some kids over at S.C. about the responsibility of the film arts." He paused. "Where were we?"

"Your wife is on two," Shirley called out from her desk.

"This will just take a minute. Hi, sweets. A benefit? For who? Since when do we belong to muscular diseases? Carmen Dragon—you gotta be kidding. I'm in the middle of a meeting. Let me call you back. I promise." He made a kissing sound and hung up. His chair tilted back so far his knees were very nearly over his head. "I want to take this middle-aged guy and age him down. I'll tell you right now it's the key to everything. Think about it. Some old guy who looks like Peter Finch. Probably his feet go to sleep at night. He has gas. He's not going to green easily."

"Green?"

"You know, dig what the girl's about. See things in a liberated way."

"He's not supposed to. I mean I think what's sexy about him is his age. His remoteness. She's drawn to that, see, rather than the other way around. I think they meet

132

sometime in the past—figuratively speaking—without even knowing it."

Lodeman placed a pencil between his upper lip and nose and stared at me without blinking.

There were a few other considerations about which Lodeman wanted my best thinking. Music was not a successful art on the screen, he thought. How about a jilted wife who goes mad? An acupuncture scene? We'd talk some more, he said.

Leaving the offices of Dedalus Productions, I thought to myself: if they can identify a corpse from its dental work, surely they had ways of recognizing a piece of written work. Something would be left. An idea? A swatch of dialogue? A flashy bit of characterization?

# 24

It had been a long day, to say the least. None of it went together. The beach, Leslie, Lodeman. I felt as if I'd been wildly ordering à la carte. I drove home through the rush hour into the throbbing sun. I was hot and tired and my head ached. I missed some turns coming off Sunset. I panicked and started reading signs instead of trusting landmarks. A man in a bakery truck unsnarled what I had done and got me going in the right direction again. A Chow raced along with my front wheels barking wildly for about a block.

Gene and Sally were not back yet. Annie was home and the maid was out in the kitchen starting dinner.

"Want to see me do 'One, two, three O'Leary'?" Annie asked, eagerly dogging my tracks.

"Not just now," I answered back—a little too sharply. I was tired and wanted to be alone. I turned to Annie to apologize, but she was gone. I pulled off my jacket and slacks and lay down on my bed. Cool currents of evening air circulated around my disheveled self. I stared at the ceiling. Understanding gathers inside me like hunger or anger. It presses for acknowledgment. You can fight it off like a sneeze or nausea, but soon it's better just to let it happen. Baby out with the bath water now: the past had eclipsed the present. Somehow the unrelieved monotony of existence had caused me to see the past, wet and sparkling, ahead of me. But it is one thing to see a mirage and another to try to drink from it. I had wanted so much to see a movie of the book, some evidence that I had gotten somebody to imagine what I had imagined. I had wanted so much for Nick to be what I had wanted him to be. I was a ridiculous person. I could feel it like scales on my body. Warts. Cataracts. I went to the mirror in the bathroom. A light tan completely disguised my infirmity. No wonder Leslie sat in the shade. Resolved: I would abort the deal with Lodeman and say a few good-byes. I like good-byes—they tear me apart, and possess a certain vulgar appeal to my sense of style.

There was a rapping at the door. Annie entered bearing a gin and tonic on a plate.

"Annie: you are terrific. Did you make that?" I asked. A soft lump formed in my throat.

She blushed with pride and offered it to me. I took a swallow. It was a brute. "You don't mess around," I said. "How about you? Aren't you going to have something?"

"Can I? In here?" she asked.

"Sure," I said and she ran barefoot from the room. She returned with a 7-Up with lemon. Seeing her across from me, I remembered myself with my mother. Myself with adults. Myself with someone older I adored. Tears sprang to my eyes. I took a long deliberate swallow of Annie's almost toxic cocktail. Was this part real? My thoughts were becoming diffused.

"Well," I said, pulling myself together, "what shall we talk about?"

Annie shrugged.

"We'd better have a proper conversation or Whosis out in the kitchen will think we're just a couple of drunks tying one on."

Annie giggled with obvious pleasure.

"Now let's see: We won't talk about school because everyone talks about school. And we won't talk about how much you've grown since I last saw you because that's just too stupid and middle-aged. And I certainly won't ask you what you want for Christmas, or if you're a good girl and help your Mommy—"

"That's just what my dentist says!" Annie laughed.

"That's what *my* dentist says."

"I know," Annie said. "We could talk about you."

"Oh, let's not. I'm a boring subject."

"Come on. Please?"

"All right."

"Are you going to stay with us for a long time?"

"No. I have to go back."

"Well—longer than 'til Monday? Because if you did, you could take me to school if you wanted."

"I'll tell you what: if I do, I will."

"*Please?*" she begged me.

I looked at Annie with a kind of horror. It was nothing to walk off with a little girl's heart. Careless flattery, just a little attention. What felons adults are.

Gene and Sally were back. We could hear them in the front hall. The family closed ranks again and I got ready for dinner.

Dinner was really excellent. To my shame, I haven't the dramatic sensitivity to lose my appetite when I'm miserable. I'd give anything to be able to languish. Sally was pouring coffee. "Oh, before I forget, Honey, Nick called and said he can't make it for tennis tomorrow.

136

Something's come up. Anyway, he'll call and make another date. Nick Ballard," Sally said, turning to me. "He said to say hello."

"Hello back," I said and looked up at Gene. Gene looked at me evenly, but made no comment.

"Nick's a funny guy," Sally said. "We've known him a long time now, but I know so little about him. He's so private. Yet he's terribly dear to Annie and me. And generous. You should see his Christmas presents! Unbelievable. He knows what we want better than we do. You know, when I was pregnant," she smiled, remembering, "he gave me a hand-blown glass pig with a little glass pig inside. I'd had trouble carrying Annie. . . . It was uncanny."

It was unmistakably a story about Nick. Something inside me dilated.

"How did you make out with Lodeman?" Gene asked.

I told him, chapter and verse. Gene took it all in without comment. He asked me a few questions about particulars. "What are you going to do?"

"Well, I'm certainly not going to let him have the book."

"Why not?"

"What do you mean 'why not'? It seemed to me we reached an absolutely perfect misunderstanding. I don't say the book was a masterpiece, but I certainly don't want to see what was good about it ruined. Besides, there are reasons why I would rather not see it made into a movie," I added petulantly.

"What are those?"

"I can't be specific. I felt very deeply about the characters—and the setting. But now I want to be rid of them," I said, voice drying up.

137

"So skip the screenplay and sell them the book," he answered practically.

"I can't do that. That's like putting your baby up for adoption."

"Let go, Kate. Take the money and write another book."

*Another* book? Did I have any other subject?

"It's the best thing," Gene said quietly. "I know this one meant a lot, but if you don't write another, this one will write you."

# 25

I read a whole book about disaster once. It told you what to do in an avalanche (body surf); when the elevator is plummeting down the shaft (jump at the anticipated moment of impact); how to deal with a shark (hit him on the nose and/or scream underwater). The author's message was: don't just die. But I don't recall a thing about psychological peril. What to do, say, when you accidentally fall in love with the wrong person. Or become hopelessly lost in the past. Cook food in a hub cap? Write HELP in big letters? Wrap yourself in newspaper and eat your shoes?

I knew I had endangered myself. Now I would have to improvise a solution. Not knowing what to do, I simply began following my instincts. I drove the next day to the Farmer's Market. It was something I had planned to do but hadn't done. So now I would do it. Simple.

The Farmer's Market is the West Coast version of Les Halles, housed in low sheds in the middle of a massive parking lot. Junk and treasure are all thrown together in narrow alleyways. It attracts all kinds of people. Well-dressed matrons come there to snack and plan benefits for the less fortunate. The less fortunate come and buy a hot dog. Hippies suck up fresh carrot juice. Small children lie zonked in their strollers while their mothers shop. Tourists stand in the middle of the alleys counting their change and calling out warily to each other. In twenty years it hasn't changed a bit.

I visited the Stations of the Cross in my sorrow—the taffy machine, the lady who makes chocolates with her bare fingers, and my Patron Saint, the peanut butter machine. The nuts went in at the top and tumbled down a chute to point B. There, discreetly out of sight, they were crushed and released to point C, a huge vat with rotating paddles. At some point, oil and sugar were undoubtedly introduced. It was the most peanut butter in one place anyone had ever seen. The Fort Knox of child food. It still filled me with satisfaction. I'd never bought any as a child. Now I could. I took out my wallet. But no. I didn't want any.

I felt as if I'd been slapped hard. So that's why my parents never bought any—maybe it wouldn't taste as wonderful as it looked.

From across all those years their kindness struck me. I'd always thought it was too expensive and we couldn't afford it. God knows it looked very valuable. They had never let me suppose otherwise. Think of that. No, don't. Why not? Not *here*. That was far away. That was long ago. You're not known here. All those key chains and sombreros. Why can't you think of these things in churches or concert halls?

But I'm never in those places. I tend to be in the supermarket, in a long check-out line, my basket heaped with items (a chorus of false claims singing in close harmony). That's when I begin to think about infinity—the

140

insignificance of me in my role as one of many—and I begin to wonder if I exist at all and, if I do, of what possible importance it is. Then I see the vanity in consciousness and feel it begin to erode. I begin to founder among life's great questions and the scouring pads. It's too much for me, I'm letting go, please won't *someone* . . .

Rammed from the rear by a shopping cart, I take up life's struggle once again.

How I wish there were some way to develop my guilts and depressions into a Tragic Sense of Life. It would lend a certain dignity to my existence. Like turning change into dollars. But you have to be able to think, and I try never to do that in New York. New York is for opinions and criticisms. They seem to go with the short, shocking episodes of daily life. You need the long connected passages of country life to sustain something handsome like Despair or Faith. Now wait, right here was the beginning of a thought . . .

Enchiladas! That's what I wanted. There was a lady sitting at a table eating cheese enchiladas with hot sauce, refried beans, cold shredded lettuce, and a nice warm humid stack of tortillas. A single lady she was, eating carefully while she read her lending library book. Her shoes and purse matched. I tried to picture her in New York at Schrafft's, waiting endlessly for a Tomato Surprise. All those old hens pecking at their softened food, slurping up Manhattans, their arthritic fingers curling around their diamonds, living off Social Security, Medicaid, and their husbands' modest leavings, hoping the optician down at the corner wasn't swindling them. Desperately hanging on to their rent-controlled apartments while the landlord audibly wished them a coronary. Con-

fiding their anguish and hopes to bored butchers loung-
ing among bloody cuts of beef.

*WELL OF COURSE IN NEW YORK THERE'S
REAL SORROW. THEY TURN OFF THE HEAT
AND TRY TO RUN YOU DOWN. YOU HAVE A
GENUINE SENSE OF REALITY, KNOW WHAT I
MEAN? SAY WHAT YOU WILL ALL THAT VARI-
ETY AND VITALITY, I THINK IT'S GOOD FOR A
PERSON.*

well, i plan to spend my sunset years in a healthy climate, and of course i'll have my lost wax class Tuesday
nights. The people out here are real friendly and out-
going and you can grow things, get to the beach, and it's
just excellent for raising children.

*TO EACH HIS OWN, I'M SURE, BUT IT'S SO
PLASTIC! AND THE DRIVING IS OUT OF THE
QUESTION. YOU PEOPLE SPEND ALL YOUR
TIME IN A CAR!*

of course i always feel so trapped in New York because
you can't get away, and all that violence would be on my
mind . . .

I ordered a Mexican dinner to go. Moving down the
alley now with a very warm paper bag pressed against
my side, I stopped and selected some peaches from a tall
velvety pyramid. I bit into one waiting for my change. It
ran warm and sweet down my chin.

Walking away from the arcades, with the sun beating
down on the macadam and parked cars, I suddenly sensed
that I had come more than half-way through something. I

142

felt myself taking hold. Something about my own food in warm paper bags, my own car, knowing the way home. It was a good feeling. I thought of Rose Kennedy, that remarkable old turkey, with her coif and false lashes, and how she knew how to live in relation to her life, not just in it. They don't teach that any more. I suspect it's the secret to everything. It's incredible that I should have borrowed from her life at that moment—vulgar of me, I know. But then I was required to eat all my succotash when I was little—because of the poor starving children in Europe. I was expert at inappropriate connections.

# 26

About to pin the tail firmly to the donkey's ear, I suddenly had a look at what I was doing. Hell, everyone knows what to do with the tail and moronic producers. And aging suitors. This part would be easy. Set off all the fuses and run like hell.

I found a bookstore near the UCLA campus in Westwood and in it a copy of my book. The clerk wrapped it with infuriating care, smoothing the corners into goody-good little triangles. Folding these, he reached for the tape dispenser. Empty. He loaded it ever so carefully and resumed his work. Now then: where was he? His order book, what had he done with his order book? He retrieved that and began to make the slip out in triplicate after a fretful skirmish with all the carbon paper tongues. His pen skipped. He rewrote everything a second time very carefully.

"Never mind the ribbon," I blurted, sensing he might truss himself in its crinkly lengths if I didn't stop him.

"Won't take a minute," he said, spreading the loops on the finished bow and zipping the ends with his scissors. "I always say: if a job's worth doing, it's worth doing well.

Have fun with it," he said, handing me the story of my life.

I knew the name of Nick's street, and he had described the house a little. I was guessing I could find it. The street lights had snuck on (I always miss the first green of spring, too). The street wound in a slow ascent, while my confidence wound down. Slow Curve. Children Playing. Beware of Dog. Sound Your Horn. Private Way. No Entrance. Stop. Exit Only. So many admonitions. Great box hedges and handsome drives, carriage lamps, and disadvantaged jockey figures in their iron silks, and big houses warmly lit inside and out—smiling distantly at intruders. Each one might be the one. Everything looked like a Pontiac ad. I hit the brake and the car jumped to a stop. I found it.

It was gray and very modern and partially shielded by a wall. The living compound lay somewhere behind. A jungle of squat palms and bushes assuaged the uncompromising geometry of it all. A beautiful pepper tree with pale green tresses, almost sweeping the ground, seemed to cool the house, gently, like a blackamoor's fan. The entry to the house was lit, a glass door leading to another glass door. More green was growing in the entry. You could see in, but you couldn't. A prowl car swung around me. A cop looked me over and drove on. I turned into Nick's drive so as to appear to be on legitimate business.

I wasn't exactly sure what I had in mind, and the house wasn't helping me any. If it had been Hallowe'en I would have taken one look and said—forget it. Nice people had organdy curtains in the window.

I got out of the car and crunched up the rest of the gravel drive to the house. I suddenly had an unbelievable desire to pee. "Nervous excretion," a friend once said to

145

me before we rushed on stage. I walked up to the glass door. Bullet lights shone down on my head. They were warm and blinding like stage lights. A phantom breeze began to rustle in the palms. The bouquet of the canyons wafted down at me. Bali H'ai, Bali H'ai, BALI H'AI! I jumped out of the lights and cursed myself. That was close. I placed the book against the front door. It slid down. It didn't look like much. ("Leave it *all* behind." "I *am*, I *am*.") My fingers curled around the shell in my pocket. It was just a small one. A little white fan, stronger than it looked. See, I had this idea maybe I could throw it into the Atlantic when I got back . . . I took it out and centered it on the package and left. And I never looked back.

Driving away was like ripping out row upon row of knitting. You just simply have to make up your mind you're going to do it.

# 27

Putting things right is like cleaning closets. Once you get going, everything goes. Whadya say we get rid of the old typewriter? I've never liked that lamp. And how about Uncle Louis while we're at it?

Having trashed the whole Nick situation and, *ipso facto*, my novel, I could scarcely wait to tackle Wechsler and Lodeman. Tomorrow might be a good day for a root canal job, have a couple of bones reset, maybe a little electrolysis. A thousand hairs removed a minute, the ads used to promise. A thousand hairs—from *where*?

Oh, I was really feeling good. When I got back to the Foxes I found everyone gone. Annie was off on an overnight with some pal. Gene and Sally were in the Valley— back after midnight, a note said.

I had the whole house to myself. Nice. I tried it out. I slipped off my shoes and walked around on those cool floors. I passed through all the rooms. Everything was so neat and put away. The aroma of Pledge and Pinesol still hung in the air. The pillows on the couch were punched and swollen. With everyone away, they were so vulnerable to me. Sally's nightgown hanging on a hook. Clinique make-up. Gene's reading glasses—they were quite strong. Memoranda in the kitchen: pool man Tuesday, Annie to Dr. Hoyt 2:30. Call Lottie re: macramé. Somebody's doodles: over and over again, stacked boxes in perspective. And a word rewritten and repeated almost like textile design in the background: danger. Danger? I like to write *Egypt* in script. For years I've tried to make it look right. All those loops make it look like tangled yarn. *Follow* is a nice word. It flows, never snags.

I unpacked my food from the bag and set it to heating on a very low flame in heavy dishes. I found the wherewithal to make a martini. I even found some nuts and got everything I needed assembled around the telephone. All comfy.

"I was just about to call you," Ron said. "But I came through the door and said to myself if I don't take a shower first I'll just pass out. This *heat*. See, I have this system that is based on actual medical fact. You take a shower, keep making it cooler and cooler. Then you get out and let the air dry you. No towels. It's the body's way of air-conditioning itself and it's very healthful for the pores."

"It doesn't seem hot to me. What is it—eighty?"

"At *least*. The weather backs up against the mountains, see, and that's it. Just hangs there. Next it'll be the August fires, then the rain. I'm telling you . . . such a drought. Then all the top soil goes. I had a friend every time there was a fire he used to run a hose from the pool to the roof and just kept wetting it down so the roof wouldn't catch. Do you believe it? This is civilization?"

"I talked to Lodeman."

"Yes, I know. He called me when you left. He's a hell of a guy, isn't he? He thought the meeting was very productive. That you made real inroads. He said you'd

148

agreed to some changes, it was just a question of developing certain things, I don't know, you'd have a better idea . . ."

"He sucks, Ron."

"What's that?" Ron asked politely.

"I said he is without any redeeming qualities."

"Oh, I thought you said—"

"I did."

"Norman Lodeman? I don't get it. Lodeman is a very articulate and aware guy. An intellectual. I think he went to Dartmouth."

"I'd bet on it."

"Wait a minute: I went to Dartmouth."

"For Winter Carnival or did you stay a while?"

"That's a very hostile thing to say."

"Then don't pass off Lodeman as an intellectual. It's bad enough he's an asshole—"

"Look, Kate, there's no reason to get excited. If there's some business problem here, I'm happy to accommodate, that's what I'm here for."

"I'm not excited. I'm really not. I'm simply diagnosing the man's condition. He has a terminal case of stupidity and the sensibility of an earthworm."

"As I recall," Ron said, back-peddling like crazy, "we had agreed that this was an exploratory session, a feeling out of personalities and perspectives. It's natural for an author to feel protective of his or her material. I'm not surprised. I've seen it before. But generally they find that these moments are even *necessary* to kindle creative juices—"

"Juices don't kindle. Juices may flow, wood may kindle. . . ."

"This is a very good deal for you, I don't know if you

realize that: I worked very hard on this. He could have asked for a professional screenwriter. Not flown you out and all that. You'll never get an advance on your next book, believe me, that will come even close to the fee you'd get for doing this adaptation."

I sat and thought about that next book, this gay assumption that a writer is just dying to do it all over again. There was no next book yet. I couldn't feel it inside as I did the last one. That quickening . . . something moving around . . . life beginning. Not arms and legs kicking, mind you, but something like bubbles in a water cooler.

And what if they took your life and did terrible things to it . . . no, let it go, let it all go.

"Sell the book." I said. "No adaptation. Tell them to get somebody else."

"You're making a big mistake. You're on the job, you protect it."

"I'm on the job, I'll throw up. Thank you, Ron, very much. I'm sorry for all your trouble. You did great. But I can't hack it."

I went outside and sat in the dark and let myself sag. I let gravity have it all. Not a muscle, not a thought to hold me up. Juniper, jackaranda, sage, eucalyptus, warm smells of California. I joined them as if I were dying. I knew when I got up that I was leaving, and would never go through all this again.

# 28

Before leaving L.A. I made a perfect act of contrition. I took Annie to Disneyland. The whole experience was like having a really bad cold when you can't taste anything, or smell anything, or hear right. Then it came over me. You weren't supposed to. We pretended shipwreck in nine inches of water, reveled with motorized pirates (Ho-ho-ho, Click-click-click) and ate international waffles. We found our way back to the car four hours later only to discover that we had parked in the "M" for Mickey Mouse section. I found that awfully depressing.

The next day I packed and shopped for a house present. I figured if Nick was going to call I'd given him plenty of time. He didn't. So fine, that put things in their proper perspective. My self-esteem would grow back after a few weeks. Right?

I returned to New York to find my plants wilted but not dead. It would take me days to read the magazines that had accumulated. The "service" had garbled half my messages, as usual. The doorman brought up some cleaning that he'd been holding for me until I got back. All in all, I'd say my life seemed to get along very nicely without me—which is either horrifying or reassuring, depending upon how you feel. Mostly, I didn't feel anything.

Summer was rapidly turning to fall. I'd missed it. I'm such a summer-lover. I've always counted the days until summer. I felt cheated. So, in addition to screwing up my life, I'd missed all the green salads, long nutritious books and shooting stars.

I entered a period of great restlessness which I tried to appease with movies, and concerts, and the company of friends. But it all made me more restless. In conversation it seemed like people never came to the point. The movies weren't about anything. Moreover, I could not sleep and could not work. Some friends offered me their house on Fire Island. They were going to close it up in a couple of weeks, but, they claimed, September was really the best time of the year. I jumped at the chance. But it was too late. The sea was too rough. The air was cold and gusting. And the sun made me edgy, appearing and disappearing behind impatient clouds. Everyone on the island was as tan as they were going to be and had given up caring. The merchandise in the shops was picked over, on sale. Lots of slacks in size 16. Sets of corn holders. Barbecue aprons that said "I'm queer for you" and tumescent beach balls. People seemed to be crowding on the ferries like refugees, as if they couldn't get away fast enough.

I hung on for a few days. I walked the beach, picked up things, then threw them away. The sand and the shells made me very sad, as if they belonged to someone else.

I collected driftwood for fires at the house. I listened to the wind during the day and the radio at night—some Long Island station announcing tag sales and missing Welsh terriers. The music was very Neil Hefti. I played solitaire on a warping table and waited for them to play something of Nick's. It was just a question of time. They did. I turned it off when the song was over.

Each night I used up all my wood so I'd have to go after more the next day. The sea was stingy, making my little charade of survival all the more absorbing.

Finally the damp turned to rain. I thought to walk to the ocean and see what it was doing, when suddenly I experienced a spasm of revulsion—the beach plumb clutching at the dunes, the hopeless erosion, the small empty houses jammed together under the scrofulous pines. I was terribly lonely. Just defeated. I threw my stuff into a bag and headed back for New York.

# 29

I'd spent half the night freezing in my own bed. Somehow in my stupor I thought I was having bad dreams. I kept turning over, trying to begin a new dream. Day broke about five-thirty. I had some orange juice and aspirin and fell asleep again. The phone rang about ten of eight, I guess. I closed the living room window and let the phone ring some more. It was damn cold for September.

"Yes?" I said wearily.

"Kate? It's Nick."

I took the phone away from my ear and held it against my chest. I was blank. Shit! *Why*? What a sloppy thing to do.

"Kate? Are you all right?"

"I'm just fine. And how are you?" I said—walking through the part.

"I've got to see you. Can you meet me in front of the Met—in about a half hour?"

"You're *here*?" Strange. I'd never pictured him in New York. "It's very early, you know, I'm not dressed—"

"I'll wait," he said briskly and rang off.

He'd wait. How do you like that? I walked over to the

window and pressed my forehead against the glass. I knew perfectly well I was going to meet him. Some people have a claim on you, and no matter what rotten things they do, you can't deny them.

I showered and managed a scalding cup of too weak coffee and found something to wear. My hair was too clean and crackled unmanageably under my brush. The hell with it. I just wouldn't look at myself. I threw some stuff in a purse and locked the apartment. I had the weirdest feeling I'd left the stove on. I let myself back in and checked. It was off. I'd known all along it was. I locked up again. I looked at my watch. At least I was twenty minutes late.

I asked the cab driver to let me out at Eighty-second and Park.

I wanted to walk a couple of blocks before I saw him. Maybe the air, which usually ran a rip tide across the broad facade of the museum, would slap me into consciousness. I'd walked this way so often, but never once had I contrived to put Nick here.

The air was strong and tart as apples. The bright morning light fell geometrically on the buildings and pavement. Businessmen with sleepy eyes and pink, shaven faces were hurrying past. A class trip was unloading in front of the museum. Boys and girls in their weekend best stood about trying not to look foolish. I turned my back and looked downtown. The wind at my back urged me to leave. I was sure if I looked now I would see Nick. I rolled against the wind and looked up. There he was. He stood above me half-way up the steps leading to the main entrance. Something about him—he looked so out of place to me. He wore a jacket and a turtleneck. He stood caged in a giant pattern of sunlight. He strained to

155

see me in a cutout of shadow. Very slowly he came toward me. We stood just a few steps apart.

"You look strange," he said.

"So do you," I said. "It's very different here," I added.

He reached out and smoothed my hair which was frantically flying across my face. He smiled as pieces kept getting away from him. His touch was so disturbing I forgot how to speak. He pulled me to him and put his arms around me. "We still fit," he murmured, rocking me very gently.

"It's cold. You must be freezing," I said, feeling how thin his jacket was. "Just a Hollywood dude, aren't you?" I said sadly.

We kissed soft and warm, a morning kiss. My breath was shallow and my thoughts were shredding. I said, "I didn't know we were the same height," and my voice broke. The tears stopped as quickly as they came.

"Let's get something to eat," he said and flagged a cab. We got in and headed for the Plaza.

"Is that where you're staying?" I asked.

"I'm not staying anywhere. I just flew in."

"Oh."

"I'm flying back tonight," he said, offering me a cigarette.

Breakfast was served on heavy linen. Small nickle-plated pots and platters started arriving. We ate in hungry silence.

"I'm sorry about the beach," Nick said with some effort.

"That's okay," I lied.

"Did you think I figured you for a one-night stand?"

"It occurred to me."

156

He sighed and shook his head. "Let's get out of here," he said, signaling to the waiter.

"How about your change?" I said, looking at what he left on the table.

"Forget it." He led me out of the dining room and we started to walk and kept walking all day. We stopped and bought him a warm sweater to wear under his jacket. He looked a little more Eastern that way, except for the giveaway tan. Up into Central Park we walked, down Broadway, across to Fifth, east on 57th, back to Fifth. I don't think it ever occurred to us to stop. And, too, we didn't seem to belong anywhere. He began to tell me about himself. He broke off sentences with a shrug or a sigh. He never finished school. Began working when he was sixteen. Home had been somewhere near Baltimore. He hardly knew his parents. Each of them had been an only child, as was Nick, so there was no family. And no question of loving. Living was all that mattered, and that was all hard work. His father deserted and Nick had to quit school and find a job. He worked in kitchens, played piano in bars, started composing in the Thirties. Then Hollywood happened and the first part of his life dropped away.

"I've spent so much time alone . . . I don't always see the connection between me and other people. I can't explain it. I'm only around at the high moments. I don't understand how people get along all day, every day. Not that I don't like people, I do."

"Were you bored at the beach?" I asked flat out.

He looked at me a moment. "In the morning, you mean?"

"Yes," I said.

157

"I didn't know what to do with you. I was scared. I—could we talk about it later?"

"We don't have to talk about it ever," I said.

"We'll talk about it," Nick said firmly.

We walked in silence waiting for the air to cool between us. I think Nick miscalculated. I sensed him looking for something to say. "Whatever became of you when you came back here?" he said.

"You mean long ago?"

"Yes."

I took my time. It was fresh ground for me. I had no rehearsed memories of that period. It wasn't even over yet. It was too recent, too raw, maybe not even very interesting.

"After California my life was broken in two—snap— like a stick over someone's knee," I began (Oh, good lead!).

"Did it hurt?"

"I don't think so. My parents worried a lot about that kind of thing. But I thought the whole deal was sort of jolly. The trip East was a blast. I really liked talking to waitresses, and the inside of motels, and snappy-looking bathrooms in gasoline stations. As for living in the East —it seemed very exotic to me. Everyone was so dressed up all the time. It was like a game in my mind. I could hardly wait to get started. I was sure I could get the hang of it. But it was like they were explaining the rules too fast. You know—a flush beats a straight, four of a kind beats a full house, fold unless you've got a wired pair— nothing lower than nines. Everyone's yelling '*wheel 'em,*' and I'm still trying to hold my cards without dropping them."

We bought a tiny paper bag of roasted chestnuts from

158

a shriveled vendor, inhaled their autumnal aroma, and threw them away as they tasted really nasty.

"I remember my first day at school," I said, chewing a big doughy pretzel covered with baguettes of salt. "They locked me in the art room. I missed the bus home. I don't see what's so funny," I said, looking at Nick laughing.

"That's a funny place to get locked in," he said, shrugging.

"Oh, yeah? There I was, in some dumb school, all girls for God's sake. Wearing a uniform. Oh, you wouldn't understand," I said glumly. "Half of them wore glasses and had their own charge accounts, for Christ's sake."

He was still smiling.

"It was two mean-looking twins that did it. Candice and Andrea. Little Hitchcock touch," I said—pleased with the thought.

"You're still mad at them?" Nick asked, smiling.

"If I saw 'em, I'd kill 'em. Still, they must have thought I was an awful freak. People from the West always sound a little brain-damaged—don't you think?"

"How about later?" Nick asked.

"Sex?" I asked him very fast.

"Sure."

I laughed. "We are skipping ahead. Do you read magazines backwards?"

"Sometimes."

"Do you read the ends of books? Before you should?"

"I have—"

"Do you tell plots to movies?"

"Never," Nick said, hugging me to him.

"Thank God. You could be rehabilitated," I said, not stepping on cracks, then stepping on all of them.

"I went with a dancer for a while. He had no mind. He

159

was a creature. Beautiful. Sex for him was like deep knee bends. A necessary progression always practiced in the same way. *Changement, changement, changement.* Well, I had danced enough myself to know you don't need a mirror to watch yourself. Dancers are incredible that way. The image passes into their bodies and they begin to make small kinesthetic corrections. When I realized he was using me that way, that he didn't know me, didn't want to, I just went crazy. I made myself sick, you know, touched bottom." We walked awhile, holding hands, saying nothing.

"Maybe people decide to be crazy; it's sort of an attention-getting device," I thought aloud. "Well, I certainly got my attention. I was full of fear, manifest fear. Phobias. I began to fear fear. That seemed to me a truly humorous situation, not to say tragic, and I pulled myself out."

"Just like that?"

"Yes, more or less—does that sound disingenuous? You know something? Once I broke myself of the craziness, I never had any trouble dieting, giving up smoking, that kind of thing. And, I started writing," I smiled, thinking back. "The very first story I ever wrote was about a girl who tried to gas herself in the kitchen reading the Sunday *Times*. It was taking forever—she got all the way through the Business section—and decided to live. Dying was too damn much trouble. It sold. Do you know something?" I said, turning to him. "I sometimes forget who you actually are. On the face of it you're much more interesting than me. You seldom talk about what you do. Do you work in your head? I can't tell from looking at you."

"Yes," he laughed, "do you?"

160

"Yes, more and more. Sometimes I cross so far over into what I'm doing, I wonder if I'll ever get back."

"You know you talk a lot?" Nick said.

"I do? No, I don't. I'm shy—aren't I?"

"You used to be," he shouted over the traffic.

The wind changed and began to whip up the trash in the streets, levitating newspapers and gum wrappers. A cellophane cleaning bag hung across the branches of a dead tree like the clouded web of a tent caterpillar. The sky began to frown. The walking wasn't fun any more. We passed a movie and decided to go in. It was something I had wanted to see. Yet as soon as we sat down I regretted it. Why were we squandering time in a movie? How long did we have, anyway? Why was he here? I couldn't follow what was happening on the screen. The words the actors spoke were systematically translated at the bottom. Words and more words. But I couldn't make my eye jump. The action was running away from the words. I began to lose control. I couldn't breathe. I was frantic to get out. Nick grabbed my coat and led me out.

I breathed in deeply on the street. "I'm sorry—I don't know what hit me."

"Okay," Nick said, obviously concerned, steering me forward down the street.

"Oh *please* let's not walk any more," I said, turning to him. "I'm tired. It's cold and dark now. I don't understand why you're here . . . honestly I don't. I seem to keep talking to keep from talking. You talk. You tell me something I don't know."

We were standing in front of a colossal office building that was hugely empty. We sat on the retaining wall of

161

the necessary fountain in the obligatory plaza. The water shivered across the surface.

"All right," Nick began. "I read your book. Did you know I was in Palm Springs when you came by to the house?"

"No. I never rang the bell."

He smiled, at the same time, examining me quite closely. "You're tough."

"Oh yes," I replied.

"The man in your book," Nick proceeded with some effort, even distaste. "The one the girl loved without his ever knowing . . ." Nick said, shaking his head slowly. "I knew, Katie." Nick looked at me to see if I had looked away. "This is all so incredible, I don't know—"

"Go ahead," I prompted, despite a burgeoning sense of fear.

"There was something about you . . . something you seemed to save for me. Maybe it was the way you listened . . . stood by."

"It's true—we know it's true."

Nick took a deep breath and closed his eyes. "That's not all. The more I saw you—the more you came into the open. You began to lure me there, too. You were no longer just a child. Yet you couldn't have understood what was happening. I disbelieved it. Do you understand what I'm saying?"

"I don't know," I said, avoiding the possibilities.

"I realized it wasn't safe to touch you. You responded too quickly."

I looked away, so ashamed of my misplaced desire, my all too previous need to be ravished. I let the tears slide down my face and laughed, head back, until Nick stopped me.

"Katie—I wanted to touch you," Nick almost whispered. He flicked a glowing cigarette into the darkness. "It was good that you moved away."

I felt myself in a slow free-fall, end over end. "You wanted me?" I said, the sound of my voice saving me from impact. "But I thought I invented you . . ." I said dully. "Was there ever a time—did anything happen?"

"Nothing," Nick said definitively.

"We didn't stand a chance, did we . . .?" I said.

"I guess not," Nick said.

"I'm not sorry."

"You wrote a lovely book," Nick said. "But you seemed so alone. I had to tell you."

"Thanks for that," I said quietly.

Nick tucked my hair behind my ears.

"That afternoon at the beach with you—"

"I remember," I said. Such a memory is like perfect pitch. You can sound it any time.

"When we made love, Katie, no one loves a stranger like that. You had always known, I was sure of it. It scared me. We were so close. . . ."

"I must have," I said vaguely. "In all those months of work, I tried to imagine you, become you, just long enough to love someone like myself."

Nick leaned toward me and kissed me gently on the mouth.

"When finally you did make love to me, I couldn't be sure—"

Nick kissed me again.

"I wonder," I said, pulling my jacket tightly around me, "what we're really like."

At last it was time for Nick to leave for the airport. I

couldn't have stopped him. It had all been resolved. We had reached an ending. He tried to leave me in midtown. It would have been the sensible thing to do. But we couldn't let go.

We managed his ticket and waited for the flight to board. We strolled. We gazed at the planes littering the runways, the service equipment speeding self-importantly around the idle jets. Sudden hellos and good-byes detonated all around us. A large family with scores of shopping bags wept and embraced in Spanish.

We had very little to say to each other. Time that didn't matter lingered: all the rest had run out. He was gone.

# 30

I couldn't sleep that night. I padded through the darkness into the living room. I brailled along the wall until I found the liquor cabinet. I felt for the shape of the gin bottle and poured some straight into a glass. At least I hoped it was gin. It was. As I walked the icy nylon of my nightie broke against my ankles and calves like water. I sat in a chair and waited for the gin to reach me. The warmth began to spread like spilled ink. I sat for a long time, gazing into the gloom. I knew there was a big hole in my life. But there was no pain. Shock, probably. I felt as you do when you lose a lot of blood. Maybe I was letting myself die. I would watch, and listen, as I always did, and learn what there was to know. Such lady-like restraint. I remembered details other people forgot. Tap, tap, excuse me, madam, but I believe you're dying.

"No!" I shouted and turned on the lights, all of them. Why should I? How did I get to be such a good loser? Why should I lose! One good reason. Just one. Time's up.

I love him. He loves me. So why the hell do we just walk away from each other? What's so impossible? Who beneath all the chasing comets gave a royal goddamn if I kept company with a middle-aged man? Or that he had the hots for some downy-armed minor a continent away, a World War ago?

I stayed up the rest of the night, the lights blazing, the radio on, and closed down my life in the East. I was shaking all over, but the idea really appealed to me. It was so extreme. So inadvisable.

I wrote notes, packed clothes, emptied the refrigerator, stripped the bed, and started making calls as early as I could. Walking back and forth through the apartment, I couldn't believe I was doing what I was doing. Yet it felt right.

By the middle of the day I was airborne again, closing the distance between the two ends of my life. I wanted quickly to get to the part where Nick would open the door and find me standing there.

# 31

The door opened. Nick looked at me for a moment, then took me in his arms. We embraced without saying a word. Then we laughed, and I started to cry by mistake, and then he kissed me so long I almost slept.

"We made a good ending—except that I didn't want to live without you any more—again."

"I didn't ask you why you came," he said softly.

He closed the door softly behind us.

"It's nice here," I said over his shoulder. "It's so quiet. I'm actually *here*."

"All the time we've lost." Nick said. "I wish I'd known you then."

"Oh, I don't think so. I got sort of fat for a while and stuttered a little." Suddenly I stopped. "Nick? Do you have any idea how terrible the last six weeks have been?" I leaned against him. "I'm so tired."

We slept most of the afternoon, our bare backs aligned. He was trying to get over New York time, while I was getting used to California time. Always we were trying to meet somewhere in time.

"Maybe we'll always be four hours apart—did you ever think of that?"

"You've got all the covers," he said.

"Nick? Who did you marry before?" I asked, peering over the bulge in my pillow.

"Marie Wyndam."

"Was she an actress?"

"Yes."

I smiled at him. "You don't give much, do you? All right then: did you love her?"

"She was an idiot," he said, staring at the ceiling.

"Am I an idiot?" I asked.

"No. You surprise me. Maybe you're very intelligent. I like the way you do things," he mused. "I think you're very strong."

"Good God—that was a regular dissertation!" I teased. "Were you married long?"

"Forever. Two years. Now give me some covers," he said.

"And don't ask any more questions," I interpreted.

"Right."

"Some time I'll have to," I said, studying his face. "You scare me. There is a distance between us."

"I'm much older than you—I've said it before."

"I like 'em old and dirty," I replied. "That's not what I'm talking about."

Nick laughed and lit a cigarette. It was my turn to stare at the ceiling now. "I'm afraid of wasting time. Sleeping with you just now, it's the first time I've really slept in weeks. I've been afraid to."

"We have time, Kate. Plenty of time. You're staying," Nick explained. We held hands a long time. "Do you want me to marry you?" he asked.

I turned my head away and nodded, ashamed of my own conventionality.

"I'm not a good husband."

168

"But I'll be a terrific wife. *Really,*" I insisted. "Don't laugh. I'm born to it. I like all that stuff. I *wish* you wouldn't laugh."

"I can't help it," he said. "You're so enthusiastic."

When we awoke the next morning I was surprised all over again to find myself with Nick. And pleased. Then I realized it must have required some bizarre act of adrenalin to pull it off (SUBURBAN HOUSEWIFE FREES CHILD PINNED UNDER STATIONWAGON). To have closed down a whole other life. Making all those decisions in a row . . .

I rolled over and looked at Nick. His face was buried in his pillow. His arms were above his head, like a captive. He was still deeply asleep. I considered touching him, then decided against it. That kind of sleeping was better than anything I had to offer. Besides, I like being the first one up.

I struck out for the orange juice and coffee without even knowing where the kitchen was. I grabbed Nick's sweater and tied it around my neck. It was chilly inside, but outside the day was sparkling bright and, oh, a garden! The carpet was squishy under my feet. Reluctantly, I left the broadloom for a cold shining floor—but it was warm. Radiant heat! Dear God, is there anything better than a luxury hotel? Warm towels, fat little soap bars, stationery in the drawers, sheets so clean and ironed you almost choke on the smell.

The living room was coolly correct and very modern. The space was vast, clean, and noiseless. I longed to do soft somersaults through the air. I touched a wall switch and all around the room lights blinked on over paintings. Impressionist oils in radiant colors, glowing like fish tanks in the gloom. The frames were like pastry. Pictures of

169

women in ballooning skirts, lying on a soft, grassy knoll, of men in boaters and soft creaseless suits, strolling a dappled avenue. A woman on a barge, her muslin sleeves rolled to the elbow, hanging out the laundry—a little girl looking on. Young girls with golden plaited hair playing hoops, a shingled summer cottage beyond. And by itself, to one side, was a Goya lithograph, a picture of a young woman gracefully fleeing from the clutches of three-winged half-men, titled *No Te Escapalas*.

I touched another switch and thirty feet of laddered fabric shuttled back on its track, leaving the room scalding with light. The garden I had seen from the bedroom wrapped itself around the living room, too. It was like a compendium of all the green things that grow. What appeared to be a Maillol nude, rounded and very substantial, glanced away. I simply didn't believe you could have all this by making "moon" rhyme with "June."

And yet, even with all these riches, there was no orange juice in the refrigerator. How could anyone drink grapefruit juice in the morning? It was positively sinister. I took the loathsome stuff out and glared at it. I got some ice out (it hatched automatically into a bin), wrapped it in a towel and struck it a mighty blow with a can of artichoke hearts. I dipped the glass into a canister of sugar and thus made an idiot margarita. I toasted the silent morning and the unknown.

It was much better when we were touching. We were safe and close and happy. We knew each other inside out. It was the outside-in part that threw us. In a way we were prisoners of our own choking need for one another. There could be no turning back because we'd already said the most important things to one another. But I think each of us was afraid the other might be secretly boring, or irritating. It's not inconceivable you could be in love with someone who wasn't any fun.

I learned right away that Nick was far more serious than I was. He had, perhaps, not enough superficial qualities. One night he was about to settle into bed with *Nostromo*—a long book of very many pages with too many words printed very close together. I had short-sheeted the bed. Not, perhaps, the mature thing to have done, but worth trying. The very last thing that would ever occur to him was that a grown person would have made a pie bed. That a man of his age, and station, should trustingly commit himself to the sheets and find them put together wrong was out of the question. I watched him lift the covers, get out and walk around the thing, mutter to himself, shake his head.

I burst out laughing. "It's a pie bed," I explained.

"Why would you do that?" he asked, utterly at a loss.

"You should have had a lot more pie beds in your life, Nicholas Ballard."

I spent the week jumping out from behind chairs and hiding in closets. We had an argument about something. I forget what, and I did penance by reading Joseph Conrad. It seems I was not serious enough.

"I have to tell you," I said at dinner, "that the Conrad is perfect. You are right. I like everything about the way he writes. I know I'm a chucklehead, but there are many wonderful things I never intend to do."

"Such as?"

"I may go through this life without ever reading *Middlemarch* or *Martin Chuzzlewit*. The fact that they exist does not fill me with shame and longing."

"How can you be a writer and not read?"

171

"But I *do* read."

"You know what I mean," he scolded.

"I see no connection between what I do and what Conrad does. I think it's better that way. The fact that we both write doesn't mean we have anything in common. Besides, reading never makes me want to write. Music makes me want to write, and people, and sometimes just a perfect opportunity—a stretch of time."

There were many conversations we never finished. I'd like to have known how Nick worked, but he wouldn't say. It seemed his gaze was unfocused, stuck on something between us. He didn't like to nail things down. More and more he had an air of preoccupation, and I was unable to anticipate what he would do or want next. It was rather nice, and at the same time, puzzling. Just when I thought we were going to do one thing, he'd do another. I was making lunch one day when I suddenly heard the piano. I called, but he didn't answer. Too bad —black bean soup with sherry and a slice of lemon floating on top. I suppressed my disappointment and ate alone outside. He worked for two hours and emerged full of good cheer.

"Hey Kate: I love you."

"That's good."

"Are you mad at me?"

"I was. But I got over it."

"I ruined lunch . . ."

"Not mine," I said patly.

"You *are* mad."

"Nope. Jealous."

He leaned over and kissed me consolingly.

"Thanks for the kiss. But I'm jealous of the concentration—not the work. I miss working. I understand not being hungry."

"You want to work?" he asked.

"Of course," I answered, then pulled back. Did he ever think otherwise?

"Fine," Nick said and smiled at me—his broad spectrum, one-size-fits-all smile.

"You don't play fair," I said irritably. "I don't know what you think. Not really. I just think I do."

"You're intelligent."

"It doesn't *help*. I've never seen you with other people, or talked about you with my friends, or seen you with a bad cold even."

"We have all the rest of our lives to disappoint each other. Why rush things?"

"Are you planning to disappoint me?" I asked.

"Why are we having this conversation?" Nick countered.

I couldn't answer.

The house threw a shadow over us as the sun went down. We sat mute and chilled. Neither of us would be the first to make the next move or speak.

"You can be really shitty," I said finally.

"Fuck off," he replied crisply.

"Oh, indeed," I said and went inside. I closed the sliding glass door. Then I locked it. I saw Nick's head turn as the lock clicked. I ran to the front door and locked it, too. What was I doing? I was scared. I ran and locked the kitchen door. I was panting. Mean bastard! Show him. Treat me like that.

I'd really locked him out and by doing so, realized I was afraid of him. Where was this leading?

"Why did you do that?" Nick asked, suddenly appearing from nowhere.

"How did you get in?"

"The door to my study."

"I'll remember that next time," I replied archly.

"Splendid," he said and walked away.

Whatever it was, it passed. At last we had really fought. And survived. I felt quite refreshed afterwards. And said so.

"You're nuts."

"As fights go, I didn't think it was too bad. It had a certain eccentric style."

"Do you still want to get married?" he asked abruptly.

"If you ask me nicely."

"I'll do no such thing. 'Anyhow'—that's your word, isn't it?" He paused. "It'll take a couple of days to get a license, blood tests . . ."

So that's what we did. We were married by a judge, a friend of Nick's attorney. A total stranger, he listened to us promise our lives away and then sped off for a late golf date.

"Call me by my new name," I said, as we drove off.

"Kate Ballard."

"I don't believe it," I said and laughed and laughed.

He kissed me at the stop signs. We put the top down and drove very fast.

# 32

The best part of being married is that it's so arbitrary. Presto, chango—you belong to each other. I was legally, actually, technically, irrevocably married to Nick. I was his *wife*. Mrs. Ballard. I suddenly owned two houses and a lot of other things I'd never had or thought I needed before: metronomes, two phone numbers, bumper pool and an electric shoe polisher.

We opened a bottle of champagne and gave each other presents. I'd designed a canvas for needlework—a black staff on a white field with the first eight notes of the song he sang to me on the beach. I had started both colors so he could see what it would be like.

His gift to me was a Pacific *tridacna squamosa, a* fluted pink seashell so large you had to hold it with both hands.

"You win," I said sadly.

"What do you mean?"

"I like your present better than I like my present."

"Don't say that—I like my present."

"Well . . . I like yours better. I don't mind—honestly I don't. You're just an ace present-giver. Some people are.

175

It just isn't fair to the rest of us. *But*, I will tell you the thought behind my present."

"I'm listening . . ."

"I wanted to do something for you. You have everything," I said, looking around the room. "Technically, you don't even need me. I mean you were doing fine without me."

"Scraping along," he said.

"So you say, so you say. Anyhow: a thought of a more serious nature. All right?"

"All right."

"After Mother died—I found a bag with some wool in it, and needles and stuff. It had belonged to her. I couldn't bear to save any clothes of hers . . . they smelled like her . . . perfume and tobacco. But this bag—it was one of those old lady things with a wooden frame. Inside was a canvas with a trellis design. In the corner was a little triangle of stitches. She had been working with white yarn, and this little patch of stitches was quite soiled. The needle was stuck in the canvas, ready to be worked. As I looked at the thing I realized she didn't know what she was doing—or what to do next. The stitch is called basket weave, and it's almost impossible to describe in words—but perfectly simple to do. I mean, there's more to waltzing than step-slide-step, right? It was like uncovering a secret about someone. I understood her frustration, her determination, and her final despair at that moment like no other. I couldn't decide whether I should leave the needle alone or draw it through for her. At the risk of losing her, I pulled it through."

"Did you do the right thing?" Nick asked.

"I'm sure I did. I think you have to fight the force of gravity. Everything pulls us down, or backwards, by example. The past is always the most compelling thing—why never the future? The real reasons for living are so individual and secret. You wouldn't want to be Beethoven, you'd end up deaf and crazy. Or Goya, for the same reasons. Poor Eleanor, Franklin was unfaithful. Poor Rose, everyone shoots her kids. Don't step off the curb, a car might come. We are cautioned against everything. I think our reason to live is the most private thing about us, and all our failures—endless warnings to everyone." My summation hung in the air like a chord, resonant and arch. "Sorry, where was I?"

"Needlework," Nick said, stretching.

"Now I'm embarrassed."

"Don't be."

"Poor beat-up metaphor—I only meant to say it was an expression of hope, and love. I do love you."

I think everyone should have lamb chops and a bath on their wedding night.

# 33

We kept our vigil for three days. And we behaved outrageously, eating and sleeping all out of order, never even bothering to dress. We watched terrible old movies on television and kept the shades drawn, even though the days outside were beautiful.

"What are you doing inside on a day like this?" I scolded Nick.

"You ought to know," he said.

I groaned and pushed him away. I surveyed the rumpled bed, the gloom, the trays of dishes and stuffed ashtrays. "Look at this," I said to Nick. He sat up and looked.

"So?"

"It's a mess. I feel like I've totally regressed. If we keep this up I'll become pre-verbal. Know what?" I said, thinking.

"What?"

"I think you should make me pregnant."

*"Why?"*

"Then we'd know I wasn't the child any more," I said simply.

178

Nick gave me an odd look. As if I'd said something in bad taste.

"Come on. Let's clean it up. What do you say? Buy some food? If we don't—know what's for dinner? Tinned pheasant and jello."

Still Nick wouldn't react.

"If you teach me to drive that machine of yours, I'll go do it myself. Then you can watch Donald Duck," I said, covering my head with my pillow. "Nick?"

"*Okay*," he said sharply, and got up.

Coming out of the house that afternoon, I felt as if we'd been hospitalized. Everything seemed louder and brighter than I remembered. The sound of the car starting up was brutalizing.

Nick took me out and taught me to drive the Porsche. We roared up and down canyons, slid on and off the freeway, parked and unparked a half dozen times. I began to like it, except for the awful noise we made at stop signs, which sounded like bragging.

"Okay," he said, "you're on your own. Get us some food."

"Name something you want to eat," I said as he got out of the car and closed the door. "I hardly know you—I don't even know whether you like your eggs fried or scrambled."

"I don't like them at all."

"See? How about veal?"

"Fine."

"I'm scared. I really don't want to go without you. . . . Oh well. Hey!" I yelled out the window, "make the bed!" But I don't think he heard me.

I felt dislocated. I had to concentrate carefully on what I was doing. "Now I am pushing the Porsche to-

ward a supermarket for food for my home in California,"
I said to myself. Sure I am. I stopped too abruptly at a
corner and threw my arm out across the passenger seat. I
used to land against that arm, not mine, when I was little.
Trembling all over, I made myself go the rest of the way
to that market, yard by yard, driving like a scared
Granny, horns honking at me, as if I were crossing that
old chasm again.

Reality, of course, turned out to be the biggest fantasy
of all. The market looked like an airport on the outside.
Inside, it looked like Eden, only more sanitary. Fruits,
nuts, meats and sweets, swathed in gleaming plastic,
abounded, row upon row. I saw a quarter mile of deter-
gents, acres of pet food, and a health, diet, or biodegrad-
able equivalent for every bottled, canned, or packaged
item displayed. Swept along by a brisk current of Bacha-
rach shopping music, I missed the veal the first time and
had to circle back on it again. A girl in a yellow gingham
pinafore ("Bobbi") checked me out. Raw milk, Boursin
cheese, French roast coffee, Danish butter, dry roasted
pumpkin seeds, placental hair conditioner, sprouted
wheat bread. I felt a lot better. Bobbi busted a hundred
dollar bill without blinking. " 'Bye now," she said, and
winked.

# 34

What I said to Nick about being a good wife was the truth. I was nifty at it. I adored playing house. I announced myself as Mrs. Ballard to the cleaners in Beverly Hills and they were splendid about it. They did not cross their eyes and stick out their tongues. They wished me a good day and took Nick's suit. Likewise, when I signed my first check, "Katherine A. Ballard," not a snort or a giggle.

I reorganized the kitchen to suit myself, and bought a few things that were missing. How, for instance, does anyone get through life without a collander and a garlic press? I got rid of Nick's electric coffee pot and bought a Chemex. That sort of thing. I started to arrange to have some stuff sent from the East when Nick stepped in and said I should replace anything I needed.

"My clothes? How about my typewriter?"

"Sure."

"What do I do about my apartment?"

"Let's use it as *pied à terre*."

"*Pied à terre?*"

"Sure. We might want to go back. See some shows. I usually go back four or five times a year anyway."

"No—it was the phrase that bothered me. *Pied à terre.* It's so—dismissive. It's my home."

"This is your home," Nick said.

"All right—*was* my home. I wrote a whole book there."

"What do you suggest we do—turn it into a national shrine?"

"No," I said coldly. "But better to get rid of it than use it as a broom closet."

"Suit yourself," Nick said casually.

"I intend to," I retorted. Retort. That's what you do when you're mad.

"I just retorted," I said.

Nick was looking at a magazine.

"Interesting?" I asked.

He looked at me irritably. "How would I know? You keep interrupting."

"Keep interrupting? *Once* I interrupted."

He sighed. "Don't you have something to do?" he asked wearily.

"Sure. I was just going out to chop a cord of wood."

Nick threw down his magazine and left the house. I heard him start up the car and leave.

The air was zinging. What *had* I done? I sat in the fading light thinking. The lights switched on automatically. An hour later I heard the car come back in the drive. Nick let himself in the house. I called to him.

"What is it?" he said dully.

"I figured it out."

"And?"

"You're bored."

"Maybe."

"So why didn't you say so?"

"What good would that do?" he said.

"Lots of good. It's no sin to be bored. I know what: let's have a party. We need to see other people."

"I give lousy parties."

"I don't," I replied.

"Okay. Do anything you like. You're probably right. I think I'll go upstairs and lie down until dinner. Do you mind?"

It was the first time I hadn't been invited along. "No," I lied. But what the hell. Maybe I needed to be alone, too. And actually it was a good feeling making dinner, and knowing Nick was resting.

I brought a paper bag full of peas and a pot into the living room. I put on some Delius. I shelled the peas and listened. *Pok, pok, pok,* the peas fell into the saucepan. *Pok, pok.* You could probably serve fifteen people buffet style. *Pok.* Maybe move that one table over to the wall. Candles. Flowers. Oh, Delius, you bastard, you break my heart. *Pok.* I'd call Leslie, Nick could call the rest. *Pok, pok.* I wonder if the New York part of my life would make a book? *Pied à terre,* my ass.

# 35

We made up a guest list that included the Otto Harburgs (an arranger Nick had worked with for years), John Hansen (a conductor), Tammy and Burt Collier (a drunk but very good screenwriter), Dave Stein (Nick's business manager), a bunch of people Nick thought would sort of fit in, and Leslie—of course.

"The only people I feel uneasy about are the Foxes," I said.

"You needn't," Nick said.

"It's foolish, I know. But I feel like I was faking around with them. Not telling them I was seeing you."

"Oh, they'll understand. To tell you the truth, I worry about Annie."

"Really? But why?"

"She's sort of sensitive."

"She adores you. And I think she likes me. In fact I *know* she does. I think she'll be happy about it. It's easy. We'll think of some way to include her. You know, make her feel special. Take her to the beach, something like that."

"We'll have her to the party," Nick said, his tone more assumptive than insistent.

"I don't think that's such a hot idea. There'll be nothing but grown-ups around. It'll go late. I'm sure she'd rather skip it."

"Don't be silly. Kids love parties. The Foxes always let her go with them," Nick said.

"They *do*? How weird."

"Why? She's an only child. And very grown-up for her age. You'll see."

"I know Annie, sweetheart. I think she's lovely. But I don't see taking kids to parties. I think it's sort of an imposition on the adults, that's all."

"I remember you liked them when you were little," he said accusingly.

How could I deny it? "Okay, we'll invite Annie, too. But I warn you, she'll be bored senseless. I know you mean yell, but you know something? Children never remember the things you do for them on purpose. I have no memory of Grand Canyon. I do remember a cashier giving me a matchbook with a Petty girl on it. You can't win."

"I gave you something when you left for New York. What was it?" Nick asked.

"Nothing," I frowned.

"Not last summer—before . . ."

"That doll," I whispered.

It took me two days to get things ready. Nick gave me a free hand with the preparations. I moved furniture around, added flowers and candles, cooked in stages for about twenty-four hours. The sound of the piano-tuner nagging at G above middle C, then G sharp, perfectly suited my mood. Were there enough cigarettes? Cigarettes. Ashtrays. Were there enough ashtrays? Cigarettes. Ashtrays. *Matches*. Were there enough matches? Finally

185

it was done. I paid the tuner and walked around the house checking. I hadn't left much time to dress.

I chose a long white jersey dress that artfully made its way about the contours of one's body in a most expensive way.

"You look terrific," Nick said at just the right moment.

"Thanks," I sighed. "I'm absolutely terrified."

"Don't be," he smiled. "I'm excited. You were right. It's a good idea. That's the doorbell. I'd better go down," he said.

I sprayed perfume across my shoulders. As the chill mist settled I felt myself standing in the door, smaller and much younger, watching.

# 36

Coming downstairs, I heard Sally's voice first. I hung back.

"Flowers! Aren't they terrific? Look Gene—everything's so pretty. You've done something different," Sally observed cannily.

"Yes, I have, I've gotten married. I'd like you to meet my wife," Nick said, summoning me.

"*Kate*! I don't believe it. Nick! Why didn't you tell us? how in the *world*," she burbled and gave Nick a big hug.

"Really fine," I heard Gene saying as he shook Nick's hand.

"This is so *incredible*," Sally said, giving me a hug. If I'd worried about the Foxes, I'd simply overlooked Sally's enthusiasm and warmth.

"Do I get a kiss?" Annie said.

Nick bent down and kissed her. "Hi sweetheart," he said, "I missed you."

"I missed you," Annie said shyly.

Leslie arrived with an unexpected escort—a very handsome actor whose name I didn't recognize because I don't watch TV much. But he behaved as if we all knew

187

who he was—and he was going to spend the evening up-setting all our expectations. He was smashed, but in control. A slight redness of the eye, and the impression that he had lost his depth perception, was all that gave him away. The rest was all show business noise.

Leslie wore Indian sandals with no soles—just a thread running around the big toe and hitching behind the ankle. Her breasts swung freely beneath a light smoke colored challis gown. She wore a very large ring on her index finger and only the bottom set of eyelashes. Purple was worked around her eyes—a very nuanced rendering of a black eye. I noted, with alarm, that her laughter was a silvery tinkle. I knew what that meant: she was working the room. I sighed and decided to ignore her until the evening jelled. I knew if I talked to her now she'd just make me mad.

As the room began to fill up with guests—names and faces wafting past me—I realized that I'd really missed people—voices interrupting each other, the subject being changed, that sort of thing. I found I could watch Nick without his knowing. Did he look different because of me? Maybe. He talked with his hands in his pockets, looking down at his feet. He looked up sharply when someone spoke to him. His smile was a grin. He ran his hand through his hair and wrecked it. In polite conversation with the wife of a friend, I saw him reach out for Annie who was standing behind him, and bring her into the conversation somehow, re-tying the sash on her dress.

Gene found me out in the kitchen chopping parsley. He stood by and watched me, stirring his drink with his finger.

"What's for dinner?"

"Cassoulet."

188

"Smells good."

"It better be—I've been at it for two days."

"Want me to chop that?"

"No, that's okay. I'll be done in a minute."

I heard his ice cube circling in his glass. I looked up at him.

"Nick the guy in the book?" Gene asked.

"Yes," I answered and flushed. There was scarcely anything I could add.

The ice cube did a few more laps. "Sally and Anne adore him, you know that."

"What about you?"

"It's a funny thing. I think women like him better than men. He really knows how to please women. Most men don't. The glass pigs . . ."

"I remember," I said.

"Annie's purple dress."

"Nick gave her that? That's right . . . I forgot."

"We see a fair amount of each other but I never get to know him any better. I can't explain it exactly."

"Well, he comes from Baltimore and he doesn't like eggs," I said, angry with Gene for the first time I could remember.

"I apologize, Kate. I wanted to say that you are the best thing that ever happened to him. With you maybe he can work again."

"Did he stop?"

"For about two years," Gene said, somewhat bewildered that I didn't know.

"Jesus," I said, looking at him.

Leslie strolled into the kitchen—a genuine first act entrance, first the deliberate inattention, then the dazzling smile of acknowledgment directed at Gene.

189

"Gene: I'd like you to meet Leslie Tyson. Leslie: Gene Fox."

They shook hands and mentioned mutual friends.

"Mmmm, cassoulet," Leslie said, sniffing and peering into the casserole. Gene disappeared when we started talking food.

"How do you know him?" she asked, tossing the salad.

"He used to be my agent. He's a friend. I was staying with his family when I saw you."

"Friends with your agent? Nobody's friends with their agent."

"Well I am."

"Know anything about him?"

"I *told* you—he's a friend. And what do you mean 'anything'?"

"I don't know—didn't I hear he was balling, you know, what's-her-name? Oh you know the one I mean, she used to be married to . . ."

"Gene isn't balling anybody," I said flatly.

"Gene Fox, right? I'm sure it was him."

"I'm sure it wasn't." That made it a stand-off.

"Okay," Leslie said, slipping quietly into a more nearly normal voice. "Are you happy?"

"No, I'm very tense. I mean just now. But you mean generally. Yes. Very. I love the man I'm married to. He loves me. That says it all."

"How old is he?"

"Oh, *honestly*, Leslie. What's with you?"

"Just asking, just asking. Sorry. Some house, isn't it? Christ. Really nice. Can I look around? Do you think he'd care?"

"It's mine, too. And listen—when you get to the medicine chest you'll find he takes DiGel. I take the Valium and the vitamins."

"You're a very hostile lady."

"You're full of shit."

"Give us a little kiss," she said, giving me a hug. "That's some bird I brought to the party. He's playing the piano. He knows about seven chords. I don't think he knows where he is."

"Help me get some of this stuff on the table, will you?" I asked, moving quickly past her with a blazing hot dish. We moved back and forth between the dining room, where I had set up a buffet, and the kitchen.

People came into the kitchen making insincere offers of assistance, then floated back to the living room. As I was getting the last of the buffet on the table, Annie followed me into the kitchen and asked if she might have a sandwich. Instantly I realized what a nightmare my dinner would be to any child, and obliged with a little peanut butter and jelly.

"Maybe, after dinner, will Nick play some music?" Annie asked.

"I'll ask him. Listen, if you get bored during dinner why don't you sneak off to Nick's study—there's plenty of paper and pencils in there. You could draw. And there's a radio, too . . ."

"No TV?"

"I don't think so . . ."

"Oh," she said.

"It's funny, when I was your age I used to love the radio, just the way you love TV."

"But what would you look at?"

"The wall," I said flatly, picking up a hot casserole.

By the time I served coffee, I was really slowing down. I dealt out the cups and saucers and sugar lumps like a croupier. I gave Nick his cup and he pulled me down on the couch next to him. He was speaking to Otto Harburg, about business of some kind. With his arm around my shoulders I couldn't get away. I felt other people's eyes on me. Nick rubbed the back of my neck. So everybody knew. Harburg gave me a look I didn't really like.

"Annie asked me to ask you if you would play," I told Nick quietly.

He smiled. "Sure. Where is she?"

"In your study, drawing."

After a while he got up and went to the piano. He set his cup down on top and sat down. No one seemed to notice him there. I felt very excited and nervous waiting for him to start. He played "Three Blind Mice" in the upper register so it sounded like a celeste. Sure enough, it flushed Annie. She stood in the door, blushing recognition. The guests laughed and clapped and begged him to really play. He must have played a dozen of his own songs, one more beautiful than the next. And Kern. And Gershwin. And Arlen.

There's something about a composer playing his own music, or any music he loves, that is unlike anything else. The phrasing is endowed with a kind of satisfaction and involvement that's missing from every other kind of performance. He remembered verses and bridges to songs everyone else had forgotten. He sang until his voice quit. It was an uncanny experience for me. The sounds that had changed my life were my life now.

The room was silent. Smoke hung in the air. There was nothing to add. Nick took a swallow of cold coffee and looked at me—no, past me.

192

"She's asleep," Nick said, nodding at Annie. She had curled up, in a chair, exiled by food, wine, and smoke.

Nick went to her and picked her up in his arms. He headed upstairs. Her small, lovely body sagged in sleep. Her dark hair swayed as Nick walked, her ankles and soft insteps not quite covered by her long skirt. Sally got up to help, but Nick wouldn't hear of it. I excused myself a few minutes later and went upstairs to see if anything was needed. When I entered our bedroom, I saw Nick kneeling next to the bed, covering Annie with a spun woolen shawl.

"Do you love me?" I heard him say.

I stepped back into the hall and leaned against the wall for support. I couldn't breathe right. Jesus, *no*! He can't. Stop him. I'd have to get word to Sally somehow.

I wasn't the child anymore.

## ABOUT THE AUTHOR

JULIA WHEDON, daughter of a migrant radio, television, and screenwriter (and sister of another), spent much of her early life in California. A graduate of Sarah Lawrence College, a Woodrow Wilson Fellow, and Harvard Drop-Out, she lives in New York City with her husband Richard Schickel, the writer, and their two daughters. Her short stories and articles have appeared in *Harper's, Redbook, Ladies' Home Journal, World, The New York Times Book Review, Book World*, and the Washington *Post.*

94  94  01  06
11   1   1   1